See Before You Die:
Costa Rica

An Aurora Night Novel

J.E. LEIGH

ISBN: 1456598872
ISBN-13: 9781456598877
E-book ISBN: 978-1-4392-8211-3
LCCN: 2011901956
3rd edition, 2012
Copyright © 2011, 2012 J.E. Leigh
All rights reserved.

This is a work of fiction. Characters and events are the work of the author's imagination. Any resemblance to real persons or events is coincidental.

Published by Places & Spaces, LLC

*To my family and friends,
for their love and support.*

*To my traveling companions,
for their warmth and humor.*

*To the people of Costa Rica,
for their friendliness and hospitality.*

*To my adventurous readers,
for taking this journey with me.*

1

A thousand places to see before I die?

I had a long road ahead of me. Especially if every time I traveled, the trip nearly ended with a first-class ticket to the morgue.

But we'll get to that later.

At the moment, I sat in my car and tried to decide whether or not to get out. My dad leered at me from the front door of his house.

It's a well known fact that every father's job description includes the stipulations that daughters must be humiliated and interfered with at every turn. My father was a military man. He treated his job description as a mission.

I knew that working with my dad was a bad idea. Traveling with him bordered on lunacy. It just so happens that I suffered from temporary bouts of lunacy. How could I not, with a father who dressed like that?

I got out of my car. "Jeez Dad," I said. "Nice shirt." I stepped into the entranceway of his house.

He hooked an arm around my neck and dragged me into a python-like embrace. "Hello my beautiful daughter."

"Dad. You're hurting me."

He released me, shot out a hand, and raked his fingers through my hair.

I ducked away. "Will you quit it? I just fixed my hair."

"Did you?" He lifted a mussed lock and peered at it closely. "You could've fooled me."

I punched him in the shoulder.

"Owwwwwwwwwww," he cried. "The pain. The agony." He staggered backwards down the hall, clutching his arm theatrically.

"Really, Dad." I grimaced at his ensemble. Unlaced combat boots. Faded camo pants. A T-shirt that boasted a huge frothy mug and shouted the word: BEER.

"Nice shirt," I said again.

He puffed out his chest, smoothed the fabric over his stomach, and strutted.

I bolted for the kitchen.

My name is Aurora, by the way. My dad's name is David. I'm not married, never have been, so I'm still stuck with his last name: Night. Don't get me wrong, my dad's great, but sometimes I don't want to claim him as a relation.

When I reached the kitchen, I was nearly washed away by a tide of trilling and squeaking Chihuahuas. I waded through, trying to reach the liquor cabinet before my dad caught up.

My stepmom, Nelle, stood over by the stove. She turned and waved a drippy wooden spoon at me. Her belly protruded — huge and round — beneath a pale pink apron. Not again.

In the Night family, this could only mean one thing.

A new Chihuahua.

A recent addition to the clan always enjoyed the place of honor — riding around the house tucked deep inside

Nelle's shirt. Sure enough, I could see one bug-eye and a set of ears that would make a jackrabbit proud poking out of Nelle's cleavage.

"Got a new rat dog, eh?"

"Oh yes," Nelle cooed. "This one's name is Sweetheart."

Jeez. I plucked a cherry tomato from the salad.

My dad caught up. The Chihuahuas pooled around his feet. He picked up his favorite, gave it a nuzzle, and set it on the counter with a pile of bacon bits. He turned his attention to me, grabbed a chunk of my hair with each hand, and tugged the two pieces towards my chin.

"Look," he said. "It's Abraham Lincoln."

I suppose if my hair was blonde I would forever be Obi Wan Kenobi.

I shoved him away. "You're such a pest."

"I'm so cute."

"No you're not."

He snaked his hands towards my hair again.

I spun to get away, tripped over a fat duffel, and splatted onto the kitchen floor. My legs flailed in the air. "So, Dad," I said. "You're packed, I take it?"

He looked down at me and considered. "Not quite." He left the room and returned a moment later brandishing a light saber.

"Dad." I picked myself up off the floor. "You aren't taking that to Costa Rica."

"I know." He sighed. "But isn't she gorgeous?" He began to extol the weapon's many virtues.

Nodding attentively, I sidled over to the liquor cabinet and dumped wine in a glass. The red elixir lapped at the rim as I made my way around the bar and into the living room. I took a sip, plunked the glass on the coffee table, dropped onto the couch, and laid my head back.

I had a problem.

Ever since I was a girl, I dreamed of seeing the world. I sat in my room every night poring over travel magazines and yearning to be a hero on an adventure. Then I discovered *1000 Places to See Before You Die* and I thought the book had been written especially for me. I lost myself inside its pages and emerged believing I could be a hero on a thousand adventures. The book inspired me to become an adventure travel writer. To me, it was the best job in the whole, wide world.

I just had one problem.

My dad, the beer-loving Chihuahua herder, had recently been assigned as my new partner. I didn't have an old partner, mind you. Nor did I want one. Well, maybe a hot, artsy photographer named Antonio would have been all right.

But my dad was definitely not all right.

"God, I'm wonderful." He beamed at the coffee table where he had constructed the Death Star out of beer cans. He knocked the whole thing down with his light saber, then disappeared into the kitchen and returned with a timer. Waggling his fingers in the air, he set out to see how fast he could put the space station back together.

I rescued my glass from the mess on the coffee table and gulped down more wine. It wasn't that I didn't respect my dad. I did. We just had different goals. I wanted to see a thousand places. He wanted to sample a thousand brews.

Of course the whole thing was my fault.

A year before, I had entered my dad in a writing contest. The next thing I knew, my boss was hiring him to work as my partner.

Our first article was a hit.

"Loved the Vietnam story," a reader gushed in a letter to the editor. "The interplay between the seasoned vet and the naïve twenty-something was great. I hope you publish more of their articles."

A naïve twenty-something. Great. That's just how I want to be known.

"Thirty-three seconds!" My dad sprang from the coffee table and rushed to the kitchen to brag to my stepmom of his prowess.

Just then, a tiny black Chihuahua clawed its way into my favorite white shirt.

2

The next morning I woke with a start.

Not to a jangling phone, or a bawling alarm, or even rays of sunlight slanting through the window.

I awoke to my dad arranging airline peanuts on my arms, legs, and forehead. The one he popped into my drooling mouth was the one that jolted me into consciousness.

I returned my seat to its upright position. Peanuts skittered into places where it would have been improper to dig them out in public.

My dad leaned against the window and pretended to be asleep.

"Welcome to Costa Rica," the pilot chirped into the PA system. The plane bounced to the ground. Mechanical things beeped and whirred. The lights flickered and dimmed. And that was the extent of our welcome.

I think when you arrive at your destination — the exotic adventure-is-waiting-for-you place you've been dreaming about from your office cubicle — the experience should be befitting of this momentous occasion. They should throw open every door and hatch on the plane, and then allow you to scamper off joyfully, grab your bags from the neat row where they are arranged alphabetically, and head straight for the jungle or the beach or the mountains, preferably in a limo with a fully stocked bar.

But no.

You must wait for the two-hundred groggy passengers in front of you to wrestle their huge rolly suitcases from the overhead bins. Meanwhile the pilot has shut off the airflow, it's ninety degrees outside, and you're in a metal tube sitting on black tarmac. Only when you finally slog out the open door can you take a deep breath and enjoy the fresh, jet-fuel-scented air.

With the modern security nightmare, you are no longer greeted by smiling friends or welcoming guides, only churning luggage machines and grumpy gatekeepers who force you to beg your way into the country with complex visas or stiff entry fees.

And still, after all of this, you must endure customs.

Five flights of people have arrived at the exact same instant and converge on the three sleepy customs officials who look at the descending hordes as if you are invading their country. You languish in line, bathrooms and coffee kiosks taunting you from the great beyond. Your one reward for all of this — the coveted stamp in your passport — is imprinted with the last of the ink they can possibly eke out and instead of Costa Rica, you have visited C a ca.

I had been through all of this many times. But this particular customs office contained something I had never seen.

My dad entered in front of me. He stopped short at the end of a long line of people. His gaze swept the room.

"Jesus," he said.

Posters papered every surface. Out of each stared a child. Teen and pre-teen girls as young as eight or nine, even a little boy. They reminded me of the children in those ads that seek donations for food and medical aid. Only these kids weren't beckoning for someone to reach out to them. The stare of their huge eyes and the language expressed by their little bodies sent a very different message: stay away.

"Children are not commodities," one poster announced. "Stop the sex trade."

My stomach drew into a knot and my breath hung in my chest. I dragged my gaze away and focused on my peach-painted toenails. They looked gaudy and frivolous.

A memory I kept corralled in a dark corner of my mind broke free and galloped around inside my head. I shut my eyes, rounded the memory up, and shoved it back into its stall.

We stood in line for an hour.

I didn't look up once.

3

A father's job description doesn't just stipulate humiliation and interference. It also demands worry.

As we left customs, my dad reached out and touched my arm. "You were thinking of Kaylee," he said.

I noted with annoyance that his voice was creased with concern. I didn't want to talk about Kaylee. I didn't want to talk about anything. "I see you found a perfectly obnoxious T-shirt to honor our trip," I said.

My dad looked at his chest and then up at me, his eyes innocent. "What?"

"Nothing. Let's get out of here."

Customs had set us free, but I had the grizzly feel of an animal caged too long and released in the wrong habitat. I pushed my way through the crowd, seeking a way out.

NIGHT

A white sign bobbed above the furied din. Across its front, the five letters of our last name — scrawled in stark black — looked strangely ominous.

Yet the man holding the sign looked anything but ominous. He bobbed up and down with excitement as his eyes scanned the crowd. As we drew closer, I thought I detected the scent of small towns and fresh places.

The man lowered the sign. "You are Aurora and David Night?" he asked.

I smiled and nodded and reached out a hand.

"Bienvenidos." The man grasped my hand and shook it merrily. "I am Luis, your guide. Come, come, you are the last. The others are already here. The driver will be most relieved." He grabbed our bags and jogged towards a group of people sitting in a square of chairs.

Luis set down our bags and pointed to a young man and woman. "This is newlywed couple from Los Angeles," he said.

The pair sat straight-backed and straight-faced and held hands with straight fingers.

"The other four are from university." Luis gestured towards a pile of arms and legs and backpacks and hoodies and sleepy faces.

One kid — he looked to be all of eighteen — grinned at my dad. "Hey, man," he said. "Great T-shirt."

My dad shot me a triumphant look.

Luis eyed his watch. "We go." He lifted our bags again and headed for the door. The newlyweds picked up their matching suitcases and followed. The college kids scrabbled to retrieve cell phones, backpacks, laptops, iPods, coffee cups, and food wrappers. The boy who had admired my dad's T-shirt pulled out a video camera and recorded the flurry.

Outside, we found Luis standing next to a small red bus. A man shouted at him in Spanish. Luis backed away from him and hurried over to us. "The driver wants to leave," he said. "We must load the mini-bus quickly." He pronounced bus as "boose."

We crammed our bags into the back of the red mini-boose. The ones that didn't fit, Luis heaped on the roof.

I hugged my camera case to my chest and eyed the sky with suspicion. "What if the bags get wet?" I asked.

Luis translated my question for the driver. The man replied with what I'm pretty sure was a swear word. Then he tossed a green plastic tarp at Luis, who swung up on top of the bus to strap it down.

It didn't quite cover the load.

Luis clambered down and shooed us onto the bus. Then the driver set off on a lurching journey through the city streets.

Besides the driver's seat and shotgun, the mini-bus contained four bench seats. I sat with my dad and camera bag in the second seat. The college kids commandeered the first and last seats — two guys in the very back, a guy and girl in front of us. Directly behind us sat the newlyweds.

Luis explained the trip. "We drive eight hours. The driver must have mini-bus back in San José by tomorrow morning. We stop only once."

No wonder the driver was so impatient.

I knew from the trip packet that this was no easy commute. We were headed for the remote southern part of the country, to a village on the border of Piedras Blancas National Park. Our route would take us across the Cerro de la Muerte, Mountain of Death, and over dirt roads to the lodge where we were staying.

Thoughts of the long drive ahead reminded me that I hadn't eaten any breakfast. I wondered if I still had any airline peanuts stored in unmentionable places.

The thing was...I didn't want peanuts.

What I really wanted was eggs. With cheese. Extra cheese. On an english muffin. And coffee. Definitely coffee. A tall, dark, hot cup of coffee.

What I didn't want was to be stuck on a bus with a group of strangers. I especially didn't want my dad there. I wanted him at home where he belonged, with my stepmom and their herd of tiny yippers.

This always happened to me at the start of a trip. This momentary panic. This feeling that I was out of my element, that the trip would not be everything I wanted it to be, that I would go home disappointed. I didn't like being in this mood, but I couldn't help it.

Maybe it was seeing the posters, or thinking about Kaylee, or maybe it was just being hungry. I leaned back and closed my eyes. If I could just get some peace and quiet.

"Hey there."

I huffed out a sigh and opened my eyes.

The girl in front of us had turned around. Her blonde hair swished over the seatback. "I'm Stacy," she said. She smacked a baseball-size wad of lime green gum as she spoke.

"Hi," I said. "I'm Aurora. This is—"

Stacy wasn't listening. She was reading my dad's T-shirt:

If you count in dog beers
I've only had one

"—my father. He dresses like that to embarrass me."

"Yeah, my dad's crazy, too." Stacy poked the bright green gob into a cheek pocket. "Course, I wouldn't dream of traveling with him."

"Smart girl."

My dad screwed up his face and stuck out his tongue.

Stacy maneuvered the gum out of her cheek. "What's with the fancy camera stuff?" She jutted her chin towards the seat-hogging camera bag.

"We're doing a story on Costa Rica for *See!* magazine."

"No way!" The lime-colored ball tumbled from her mouth. "That's like my mom's favorite magazine. Wow. I can't believe it." She jabbed the kid next to her. "These guys are doing a story for *See!*. Can you believe it? That's so cool. I've got to text my mom." Stacy turned her attention to her cell phone. Her excited movements ping-ponged the green goo into my lap.

"Serves you right," my dad said.

Already, I regretted this trip.

4

The gas gauge sat firmly on E.

Four agonizing hours had passed. Everyone had lost the energy to talk due to lack of sustenance. The only sound that rivaled the whish of the wheels and the drone of the engine was the growl of our stomachs.

When the gravel of a parking lot crunched beneath the bus's wheels, the eight of us mustered enough energy to send up a wild cheer. Everyone fought to be the first out the door as it swooshed open onto fresh air and freedom. Bumbling out, we buzzed to the restrooms like bees to a hive.

My dad ambled across the lot and peed on a tree.

I decided against shopping with the others. Instead, I grabbed my camera and went to the overlook that fell away from the back of the roadside shop. After hours spent trapped inside of traveling machines, I found the hush of the overlook delicious.

The sun had already started its downward slide. Dark shadows lay in contrast to the glare of midday. The Mountain of Death seemed at peace today, but I knew that it would not take long for things to change. Such is the way with nature. Such is the way with people.

A breeze lilted up over the low rock wall that wrapped around the overlook. I stepped across the stony barrier and lifted my camera, shifting the lens's focus to find the perfect view. I perched on the edge and luxuriated in the happy silence.

A familiar voice pushed into my consciousness.

Aurora. For the love of Pete. Take the picture already.

I lowered my camera and smiled. How many times had Kaylee said that to me? I widened the angle on the lens. Raised the camera. Reframed the shot. Rows of coffee plants striped the valley below. Wisps of clouds ribboned the sky above. The ribbons and stripes met at perfect right angles, as though brushed on by a painter to create perspective and depth. The converging lines drew me into the scene.

Kaylee went there with me.

You know something, Aurora? Costa Rica is called the last country the gods made.

You always were a know-it-all, Kaylee. I give — what does that mean?

Costa Rica's land is newer than the rest of the Americas. It bubbled up out of the ocean a few million years ago, bridging the North and the South. It's part of the necklace of volcanoes and faults that's draped around the Pacific Ocean.

The Ring of Fire.

That's right. The Ring of Fire. And even though Costa Rica is itty-bitty — no bigger than the state of West Virginia — the country brims with five percent of the world's plant and animal life.

Sounds like a lot of bugs to me.

*Oh, don't be such a wimp. I like to think that's why they call it Costa Rica — the Rich Coast. It's positively bursting with life. Can't you feel its energy, Aurora? Sense its power? This place is so rich and new and active and **alive**.*

Yes, my friend. But you are not.

I let the camera sag. How could I possibly capture the richness of this new land, this primal place of teeming jungles and restless volcanoes? A country surrounded by the vastness of two oceans and providing a tenuous connection between two halves of the world?

What was it about this place, anyway? Why did it make me think of Kaylee? And why had I longed for this assignment more than any other? Were there two halves in me that needed to be reconnected? Did I yearn to feel new and active and alive again like the place itself?

Just take the picture, Aurora.

I lifted the camera and pressed the shutter. The lush landscape transformed into an impersonal matrix of pixels and dots.

A shout from my dad jerked me back to the waiting bus.

5

The other passengers looked guilty.

They came back to their seats toting weighty paper bags. While Luis did a head count, the seven other passengers tossed nervous sidelong glances around the bus. They acted like a bunch of naughty kids trying to divert the attention of the adults by being overly quiet and well-behaved.

I searched my dad's face for a clue. He merely smiled.

The mini-bus lurched forward.

I leaned against the window and tried to bring back the moment on the overlook. The landscape flitted by the window like images on a TV screen. Color streaked across the glass. Reflections flickered across faces. Squares of light slid across the seats, the walls, the ceiling.

Kaylee was as ephemeral as the light.

"Pura vida!" The shout rose from the back of the bus.

The mystery bags unfurled, cellophane wrappers crinkled all around, and the aroma of stale chocolate and potato chip dust filled the air. Unhealthy snacks to be sure, but they didn't seem to warrant the guilty looks I had witnessed earlier.

A pop.

I peered over the seatback at the couple behind.

The new husband arched an eyebrow at me. His lips curved into a mischievous smile. His wife sat rigidly beside him, her lips pressed tightly together. She watched as her husband lifted a can of beer in a toast.

So here was the cause of the guilty looks. Frosty six-packs of *Imperial*, a popular Costa Rican beer.

My dad handed me a can.

Empty.

He popped another. "A man could die of thirst on this bus," he said and chugged it down.

I shook my head. "Do you actually have anything to eat in that bag?"

Hours passed.

The floor of the bus rattled with twenty-four empties. We'd long since left the pavement. The mini-bus jounced along a primitive dirt road.

Stacy squirmed.

"You okay?" I asked.

"Too much beer," she whispered. "I gotta pee."

Oh boy. Her look told me she knew as well as I did that not even if the whole Ring of Fire erupted at once was the driver likely to stop.

"Hang on," I said. "I think we're almost there."

A commotion dragged our attention away from tiny bladders and grouchy drivers. The two guys in the back seat had consumed most of the beer. Now they cracked jokes and shoved each other around.

One of them pulled out the trip itinerary. "Hey, check it out," he said. "We're going white-water rafting." He waved the sheet of paper in his seatmate's face. "I bet I'll be a natural. I bet after this trip I'll be able to go pro."

"Pro what?" his buddy replied. "Pro asshole?" He ripped the itinerary away. "Hey, what's this? A canopy tour? What the hell's that?"

"Oh, you're gonna love that," the first kid said. "You'll get to crawl around the tree tops with all the other monkeys. Who knows? Maybe you'll find some long lost family members up there."

The shoving match resumed. A moment later, the video camera I saw in the airport appeared.

I returned my attention to Stacy. She rocked back and forth, exuding misery.

Finally, she could stand it no longer. She begged Luis to stop the bus. The willing guide tried to convince the driver.

It was to no avail.

The driver issued a stream of angry words, waved his hand in front of him, and slapped it back down on the steering wheel. He increased his speed dangerously, but did not stop.

Stacy shot me a pained look, scooted to the edge of her seat, and crossed her legs.

"Death in Costa Rica." The words came from the back of the bus. I turned to find one of the guys holding a beer can up like a microphone. Speaking to the video camera, he intoned in a news-reporter-like voice, "We're reporting live from Costa Rica, where a college co-ed fights for her life as she partakes in an exceedingly dangerous and wickedly pain-inducing Can-I-Pee tour."

Stacy ignored him. She fixed her gaze on the dirty front window and leaned forward, as though trying to escape the boys and propel us closer to our destination.

Then — like a bird in a bush — she startled.

I floated across the seat and into the side of the bus.

My leg mashed my camera bag against the steel wall. My dad crushed into me from the other side.

The front end of the bus veered to the right.

The back end fought to catch up.

Tires skittered over gravel and dirt, trying to regain purchase on the rough road. Brakes pealed in protest against the heel of the driver. Wheels grabbed at the road. The seats jolted. The frame shuddered.

All motion ceased.

I peered outside for a landmark to anchor my senses. But we'd passed into an alternate reality of billowy dust and cloudy uncertainty. The still-running engine whined. The now-quiet passengers breathed.

An interminable moment passed.

Then the side door slithered open. Flip-flops padded away. Stacy vanished, dust swirling over her like steam from a hot shower. Luis's door clacked open and he, too, disappeared.

We leaned forward, the rest of us still on the bus, moving in unison, watching for Stacy or Luis to reappear.

But as the dust began to dissipate, we saw a person materializing and perceived that it was someone rather different from whom we expected.

6

The rain was late this year.

That's what gave the dust an upper hand. It swirled relentlessly, refusing to release its hold on the air. The person in the road was not Stacy or Luis — that much we were sure of — but because the rain, now already a month overdue, had not yet returned to tame the dryness, the dust was allowed to keep its secrets.

Costa Rica does not have a spring–summer–fall–winter, only a rainy season and a dry season. "Dry" is a misnomer; it rains year round. But the drenching torrents of the rainy season typically begin in May and continue through November. Now a few days of the tropical sun beating on the road was all it took. The dust stubbornly held its position until a stern breeze took charge and drove the offending particles away.

When the air cleared, we could see — standing just six inches from the red metal of the bus — the figure of a little girl. Eight or nine years old, brown hair, white shirt, green shorts, strappy sandals, a pink barrette. Everything about her was ordinary.

The only thing unusual that might give a clue as to why she was standing there — in the middle of the road — was what she held in her arms.

"What happened?" Stacy came back and climbed into her seat. "Is the little girl okay?"

"I think so," I said. "Luis is with her."

"What's she holding?"

"Beats me. Looks kind of like a piglet."

"That's not a pig," my dad said. "It's not pink."

"All pigs aren't pink," I said.

"Can't you see what's in front of you?" My dad said. "Check out the pointy nose, the whiskers, the huge ratty eyes. That's a rodent."

Luis took the strange creature from the girl's arms and hurried to the bus. Hoisting himself into the front, he kneeled in the passenger seat and conversed with the driver.

Whatever he said, it angered the man.

Luis faced us. The animal in his arms tried to wiggle free. Now that it was closer, I could see that other than its size, it didn't look like a pig at all. I could also see that its beady black eyes were filled with fear.

Maybe it knew something we didn't.

"We reach edge of village," Luis told us. "I am sorry, but I must take the girl — she is my daughter, Rosa — I must take her home. The lodge is past village. The driver will take you."

Eight pairs of eyes turned with apprehension on the man behind the wheel.

"Do not worry," Luis reassured us. "You will come to a fork in road. Follow the right fork. It will take you to the lodge. You will be there in few minutes." Luis hopped down and went back to his daughter.

I wished I could trust in his certainty. For one irrational moment, I wanted to call out to him, to tell him to stay, to bring his daughter and the critter with us, to make sure we reached the lodge.

I rattled my head. I was being ridiculous.

The bus leaped forward. The driver had not learned from the close call, the tragedy that would have occurred if the bus had skidded another six inches. But soon he would be gone, throttling away from us, making his way back to the city.

I just didn't know that would be sooner than I thought.

Through the window, out towards the west, I glimpsed the horizon. Thick curls of black roiled above the silver edge. The rain was coming.

Stacy squealed. She pointed towards a fork in the road, the right prong of which we were sailing right by.

We all looked around the bus at each other. Did the driver notice? Did anyone speak Spanish?

"He'll figure it out," my dad said.

The driver slammed on the brakes.

The eight of us lurched forward. We saw what he saw.

"Oh no," I said.

"He'll turn around," Stacy said. "He has to."

The driver kicked his door open and jumped out of the bus. He circled around to the front. My dad slid open the side door and everyone got out.

The driver stabbed his foot at a rotted plank of wood that was stuck under the front wheels of the bus. The plank broke free, plummeted down a shallow gorge and splintered on a rock. A fast-moving stream swept the splinters away.

More rotted boards were cobbled together across the cut in the road, forming a bridge just wide enough for the bus to pass, but clearly in such a state of disrepair that it was no longer used.

Hence, the right fork.

"He's not going to drive across that, is he?" These were the first words I had heard the new bride say.

No one had an answer.

7

The driver pulled the bags — in one toppling tower — out of the bus and onto the road.

"What's he doing?" someone whispered. "Is he trying to lighten the load?"

Stunned into a stupor, we watched as the driver climbed up on top of the bus and cut the tarp free with a knife. He sent the green plastic flying. It fluttered through the air like a leaf falling from a giant tree. With a powerful kick, the driver sent the rest of the bags plunging from the roof. He climbed back into his seat and slammed his door.

"Oh no," Stacy said. "He's going to leave us."

We dove into the bus and scrambled to retrieve our things. We were only out for a millisecond before the driver screeched the vehicle into a sharp U-turn. The side door still yawned open. Empty beer cans shot out as he swung back onto the road. The last thing we saw was a large red square disappearing into a storm of dust.

"What are we going to do?" the bride wailed.

Again, no one had an answer.

We cast stupidly about for what seemed an eternity.

Then the military training in my dad took over. He organized us. Helped us shoulder what we could — backpacks, purses, duffels. The rest he had us pile on the green tarp. He told us where to stand. Spread the weight, our strength. We curled our fingers into the tough plastic. Lifted. Pulled. Rested. Lifted again. Made our way back to the fork in the road. One mile to the lodge a sign said. We inched along. Swapped sides when one arm tired. It wasn't so bad.

"At least the rain held off," I said.

"You just jinxed us," someone grumbled.

"There's no such thing as jinxes."

A single drop of rain pelted my nose. Then fifty-thousand. It was like someone scooped up a sky full of the Pacific Ocean and dumped it on us. The rainy season's arrival honored ours.

Things became much harder. The loads on our backs soaked, grew heavier. The road ran slick with mud. Water pooled in the tarp until my dad pulled a pocket knife from his duffel and slit the plastic, allowing it to drain.

Thunder rumbled low across the sky, echoing a despair that brewed low inside my chest. Raindrops drizzled through my hair. Raindrops trickled down my neck. Raindrops streamed over my face. My mood steadily followed the rain down.

With each plodding footstep, troubles loomed.

Kaylee was there. Then she wasn't. My dad. Beer cans scattered over the coffee table. Chihuahuas clawing. My dad intruding on my career. The posters in customs. The road. The rain. The bus. The driver. The girl. Rosa.

I imagined her standing there, in the middle of the road, staring us down with those huge eyes, willing the bus to stop. She held the creature in her arms with a fierce protectiveness. A fierceness she must have inherited from her father, who rushed to her side, gathering her to him, holding her in his arms and thanking the god of buses and fathers and little girls.

Thanking that god for letting her live.

I looked at my own father. When was the last time we shared a moment like that? There was a time, I knew, when I adored him, perhaps when I was Rosa's age. Why now did every interaction end in annoyance and a burning desire to escape, to be alone? Why did every word, every gesture, every look go wrong? Was this the inevitable course of relationships, to move from adoration to annoyance as the years slide by?

Or was it just me? Was I some sort of failure? At family? At friendship?

Kaylee knew.

Is that why I was nearly thirty and still flitting about the globe, seeking something — *what?* that I wasn't finding at home. Was I destined to be another restless thirty-something who couldn't fall into the regular pattern of life?

Take care, Rosa. You will grow up. The things and people around you may not change much, but you will. You will end up wandering a long road in a foreign land with the rain beating down and the people around you strangers.

My dad smiled at me then. He pointed ahead and

through the rain I saw a thatched roof rising like a mountain out of the swirling clouds. And closer still, a sign:

PIEDRAS BLANCAS LODGE

We were there.

The rain lightened and the sun shoved the clouds aside and shafts of light speared down on the path before us. And in that moment the people around me did not seem like strangers, but more like friends. We had pulled the tarp through the storm together and now we smiled around at each other and the lodge beckoned like a home fire, and the place was no longer foreign, but filled with an affectionate mist that steamed off the ground and curled around us, welcoming us to this rich and living place.

I smiled back at my dad.

We were there.

8

Everything about Grace fit her name.

The young manager of the Piedras Blancas Lodge turned to ask someone to fetch towels for us and I saw that her hair was no exception. The lavish locks tumbled down her back and swirled around her hips like a shimmery black waterfall.

Grace listened with growing concern to our tale of pouring rain and reckless drivers and missing guides and lost little girls. She assured us that such a thing had never happened before.

The towels arrived. The soft terry fluffed up both our sodden hair and dampened spirits. We left our bags dripping at the entrance and followed Grace into the heart of the lodge.

Fashioned from twisted wood and feathered palms, the open structure sheltered us from the rain like a giant gazebo. A railing wrapped around three sides. On the fourth side, a wall masked the kitchen. Grace led us through a maze of couches and chairs. She stopped near a checkerboard of tables.

The scent of food melting and steaming and grilling and frying wafted out of the kitchen. I looked with longing at the tables and wondered when we'd be able to eat.

"Sixty-thousand." Everyone in our group squinted up at the thatched roof and nodded appreciatively. I realized I hadn't heard the question. "The roof," Grace said, smiling graciously at me, "is made of sixty-thousand palm leaves."

I flushed at my obvious lack of attention. I was, after all, the one who was supposed to be writing an article.

As we circled back to the entrance, Grace lifted her slim hand and pointed outside. "This," she said with pride, "is our new hydro-electric system. It supplements the power here at Piedras Blancas Lodge."

We peered over the railing at a cement chute that ran down the hill and dumped into a large pool. "As the water rushes down the chute, it charges a bank of batteries that powers our generators. The best part," Grace said, "is that it doubles as a water slide for our guests."

My dad's eyes gleamed like a boy who had found an unattended beer keg.

The tour ended where it started. Rooms were assigned, keys handed out, luggage sorted.

"One last thing," Grace said. "Don't be alarmed by the alligator."

Everyone stopped.

"His name is Tico. You will pass by his pond on the way to your rooms."

Nobody moved.

"He's a caiman," Grace explained. "Not a big one. Two, maybe three feet long. Don't worry. He likes guests."

Yes. I'm sure we look quite tasty.

"In fact, that's how he got his name," Grace said. "The people of Costa Rica are known as Ticos. And one day, our caiman decided to belly up to the bar here in the lodge. One of our guests said the alligator wanted to drink like a Tico." She shrugged. "The name stuck."

Great. What if Tico the friendly gator decided to belly up to my bed?

Reluctantly, we left the lodge and trooped up the hill towards a cluster of bungalows. The path skirted a small pond. There Tico-the-gator lounged, his caiman eyes and nose peeking out of the water. Watching.

I could have sworn he fixed one eye entirely on me. What he did with the other eye I wasn't sure, but I had the feeling that Tico and I were not going to be the best of friends.

Twenty minutes later I left the room and braved Tico's lair to go back to the lodge. My dad was already there. I could hear his gleeful hooting well before I reached the front steps. What I wanted more than anything was food, but like the parent of a wayward child, I had to find out what my dad was up to.

I found him at the top of the water chute. He lay back in the slide with his hair sticking out in gray tufts, belly bared, bony legs together, arms crossed over his chest.

I smiled in spite of myself. He could be so annoying and meddlesome, yet his approach to life was infectious. He believed that people shouldn't take things too seriously. His carefree outlook had a lot to do with his experiences in Vietnam. For as long as I could remember, whenever life's complications arose, my dad would simply shrug them off and say, "At least nobody's shooting at me." Nothing fazed him.

There was just that once. The only time in twenty-nine years I remember seeing him upset. The day my dad cried.

"Wheeeeeeeeeeeeeeeeeeee." He hit the water like an asteroid, smashing a massive crater into the pool.

"Dad!" I hollered down to him. "You better cut that out. There's not going to be any water left in that thing."

He squinted up at me. He wore a pair of Chihuahua boxer shorts that clung indecently.

"For crying out loud, Dad. There's a reason they make swim shorts."

He sloshed out of the water, plucked up his clothes, and sauntered behind a banana tree to dress.

A knot of people gathered near the lodge's kitchen, enticed by the hot scent of garlic, oregano, cilantro, and pepper. Two cooks emerged from the kitchen. They bore rounded bowls of black beans and rice, or *gallo pinto*, a Costa Rican staple.

They darted into the kitchen and brought back meat, onion, and red peppers piled on skewers; slices of succulent pineapple and melon fanned over a plate; steamy corn tortillas folded into a warm cloth; fried *platanos* — a kind of green banana — heaped on a platter; and dark bottles of a cool red wine.

Their work finished, the cooks vanished.

A startling young man appeared to take their place.

9

The man needed tall words to describe him.

Lascivious and narcissistic came to mind.

As the man looked over the newcomers, his eyes devoured the juicy bits of all the women. His gaze lingered on Stacy's breasts for some time but passed right over my less-than-impressive set to take in my hips.

Despite his rude ogling, he seemed to think that we should find him infinitely more impressive. He flicked his long, freshly-brushed blonde hair as though he had just emerged from a salon. He left his chest bare so we would have the honor of availing ourselves of his physique. He shifted every few minutes, settling himself into a new pose and quietly flexing his muscles.

"Well — if it isn't Fabio himself," my dad said.

"No." Stacy giggled. "This is the jungle. That's Tarzan."

"Stop drooling," my dad said to me.

"Please." I detested the guy on sight. Did something sinister lurk beneath his blond and sunny exterior? Or was hunger starting to affect my imagination?

The Tarzan-man flashed us a cool smile. "I love fresh meat," he said.

I wasn't sure if he was talking about the dinner or us.

Tarzan joined the group and leaned in close. "You ladies are lucky," he crooned. "I'll be guiding your raft trip this week. You're in for quite a ride."

I finally had a plate in my hand.

Stacy was in front of me digging a spoon into the fluffy soft rice when I experienced a familiar sensation. It was exactly that feeling you have when you're settling in to enjoy a movie and the Girl Scout cookies beckon from the top cabinet on the right where someone hid them behind the flour. You can't see them or smell them or hear them but you know they're there just the same and you have to get up out of your nest on the couch and go to them. Well, that was the feeling I had just then and I had to take a look.

What I saw was better than cookies — a tasty, mouth-watering, savory, scrumptious, delectable, yummy, delicious-looking man. Beckoning like a towering chocolate lava cake with a molten center.

Just perfect for digging into and—

Aurora! Snap out of it. Clearly you've been deprived of food and chocolate way too long.

Now look — is he staring back at you? No, I think he's hungry, too. Must be staring at the rice and beans. Now he's smiling.

Wait a minute. Do men smile at beans?

I settled between my dad and Stacy, my plate heaped high and steaming. The jungle hung close all around.

The companionship of the people circling the tables buoyed the sixty-thousand palm leaves. They seemed to float on our contentment. A slight change in the pitch and tempo of the chatter made me aware of an addition to our party.

Luis and Rosa entered the lodge. Grace swept them into the fold. Rosa held a bundle of palm leaves in her arms and as Grace accepted them, I had a fleeting vision of us sitting up under the night sky, weaving them into the roof.

Then Tarzan was beside Rosa, a hand on her shoulder, leaning in close to listen to something she said, guiding her to a chair, bringing her a plate.

Next, I glimpsed the lava-cake man again and my face flushed. I convinced myself that it was the heat of the food or the warmth of the company. I nestled back in my chair and took a sip of wine.

We were really there.

A short time later, the cooks emerged and whisked away the plates. The party fragmented, the bits and pieces drifting through the lodge and settling into couches and chairs and on the floor. Our group floated to a corner where Luis and Rosa sorted the bundle of palms. They stripped the leaves until they looked like the fronds I remember twisting into crosses at Sunday school as a child. Wondering what was going to happen, I slipped my camera from its case and kept it ready.

Luis picked up a frond and deftly split it down the center with his thumbnail. He twisted and looped the two pieces into a row of loose knots. The knots formed a little braid about the length of my index finger. Luis pushed the leftover ends of the frond through the last knot. The tips waved in the air like the feelers of an insect. He held up his creation. "Grasshopper." He broke off two spaghetti-thin pieces from the spine of another palm leaf, bent them in the middle, and pushed the four ends through the knots that formed the grasshopper's body. Now the leafy little creature had legs.

Luis distributed the remaining fronds among us and it was clear that we were to make our own grasshoppers. Luis and Rosa patiently guided us and gently corrected us. Our group dissolved into a mess of frustrated giggles.

"Mine's terrible," Stacy complained.

"It's *el gordo!*" Fat. The college boys covered their ineptitude with good-natured taunts and insults.

I raised my camera and shut off the flash. I composed several shots, relying solely on the lights that flickered from the uneven power provided by the generators. I liked the effect of the faces in the shadows, the childlike joy of grown-ups taking time for arts and crafts. I focused on Rosa, the little girl completely absorbed in transforming the frond into something new.

She reminded me of why I traveled, why I wrote, and why I was compelled to tell stories. I loved writing about the places that travelers dreamed of seeing, the people they longed to meet, the foods they craved to taste, and the adventures they yearned to experience. I didn't review restaurants or rate hotels, I wrote about the lives and the families and the communities that made a place unique.

Every place had a soul — a spirit — and that's what I was there to find. That might include the thrill of a rafting adventure or the peacefulness of weaving a grasshopper. I liked to think that every place was a story — the earth the stage, nature the setting, the local people the characters. My job was to transcribe the story so others could read it, and see it, and feel like they were living it.

Of course, as in any story or any place, not all of the characters were heroes. Some were ordinary, some were villains. It was the variety of personalities that made a place and a story interesting. It was the unraveling of the secrets of a place that for me was the ultimate mystery.

In that moment, as I watched Rosa, I was filled with the certainty that I had found this story's hero. What I didn't realize was that before the story's end I would also find a villain.

10

Double occupancy.

The price for most packaged tours is based on double occupancy. The term is just plain evil when you're twenty-nine years old and traveling with your dad.

Before I went to bed, I pushed the two twin beds in the room as far apart as possible. That didn't stop me from waking up five times during the night to my dad's raucous snoring.

Now the cruel sun poked at me. I tugged a pillow over my head. As I entered a conscious state, I became aware of the shower running. I peered at my dad's bed. He'd made it by dumping the covers in a heap. I looked around for a clock. Someone rapped at the door.

The shower still drummed away, so I heaved myself up and shuffled to the door. I turned the lock and dragged it open.

Lava-cake man stood there, looking more luscious than I remembered. He gazed down at me with an amused grin. I could only gape, staring at him like a child at the window of a gourmet chocolate shop.

He spoke. His voice was just as I had imagined it — like cocoa butter, smooth and velvety and rich. "You left your camera bag in the lodge last night."

I was shocked. The equipment inside — the digital Single Lens Reflex camera, the lenses, the extension tubes, the filters — was my joy. How could I have left it? "Thank you." My voice came out in a croaky stammer.

Lava-cake man's grin grew wider.

I suddenly felt like the last Samoa cookie lying on a plate. The one a hungry man wants to snatch up, but turns away from out of politeness and self-discipline.

"Con mucho gusto," he said.

"Huh?"

"With much pleasure."

"Oh."

Lava-cake man strode away.

A tiny part of me wanted to call out and say, wait a minute! I've been on this plate for a while. Go ahead. No one else is reaching for me. But as he strolled down the path that wound through Tico's lair, it occurred to me a cookie that's been sitting out too long is probably stale.

I closed the door behind me. As my gaze raked over the bed I had just abandoned, it occurred to me exactly how stale I must look. I scooted across the room to the mirror and let out a scream.

My dad rushed out of the bathroom. "What's wrong?"

I scrutinized my image in horrified silence.

A ratty T-shirt hung limply off my shoulder. A pillow

line meandered across my forehead, down my cheek, and all the way to my chin. My hair rivaled the grand finale at a fireworks show. Worst of all—

"You okay?" My dad interrupted my stupefied goggling. "Who was at the door?"

"Oh — just — someone. I left my camera bag at the lodge."

"That's not like you." My dad gave me the once-over. "You do realize you're not wearing any pants, right?"

I do realize. That's the worst-of-all part. I scooted over to my bed and fished out the shorts I had shed during the sweltering night.

"So what do you think?" my dad asked from across the room.

That question usually preceded something embarrassing. I turned. Yup. Embarrassing.

"Jeez Dad. Where do you find those T-shirts anyway?"

"You're the one that introduced me to the internet."

Way to go, Aurora. I looked at his neoprene raft booties, the wet suit he wore rolled over at the waist, the gloves with fingers that were pre-curled to fit around an oar, and his quick-dry T-shirt:

My wife asked me to pick either her or rafting
Man, I sure do miss her

"I bet Nelle just loves that shirt."

"She jumped me when I modeled it for her."

"Yuck. You do realize that when we go rafting it's going to be like five-hundred degrees with one-thousand percent humidity, don't you?"

"I'm combat troops. I prepare for every contingency."

"Right."

"Aren't you going to be late?" he asked.

"Late?"

"The spa," he said.

"Crap. What time is it? Where's my watch? I'm such a disaster. I can't believe I left my camera bag at the lodge." I grabbed my toiletries, dashed into the bathroom, and tried to shower into a new day.

A few minutes later, I stood before the mirror in the room. I picked up my hair dryer and shot a blast of heat at the wet mess on my head. My normally nice, wavy hair burst out in a puff of frizz. "Dang humidity." I dug in my bag for a scrunchie. Then I wrangled the curls together and twisted the elastic cloth around the mass of hair.

"I'm going to breakfast," my dad said. While I was in the shower, he had changed into shorts — a scary sight — and a blessedly plain T-shirt.

Now, on his way out, he pranced by, lifted the poof of curls at the back of my head, and said, "You do know what you find under a pony's tail, don't you?"

I marched down the path from the bungalow and marveled at the jungle's morning show. At home I lived in a desert where the plants, cowed by the sun, looked submissive in their muted earth tones and soft pastels.

Here, the jungle towered defiantly against the sun. It shone with a shocking green. In the shaded areas, the green glowered an almost black, but where light touched the vegetation, it glimmered electric and neon.

I strode through the jungle, half expecting a T-Rex to come crashing towards me.

Costa Rica was, after all, the setting for the movie *Jurassic Park*. A hundred or so miles off the Pacific coast, the island of Isla Nublar was where a couple of velociraptors and a cranky T. Rex made Laura Dern have a really bad day.

Something slithered near my foot.

I yelped, leaped sideways, hung my foot on a vine, fell over backwards, tumbled off the path, and landed with my legs in the air.

I struggled to sit up and glared across the path at Tico-the-gator. He grinned toothily at me.

"You think that's funny, do you?"

He slithered into his murky pool.

"You better run."

Tico immersed down to his eyeballs.

"Talk about prehistoric." I picked myself off the ground, plucked a few trees from my hair, and tried to brush the green stains off my clothes. "Perfect." I glanced around, embarrassed.

I caught sight of Grace in the lodge. She wasn't looking my way. How I envied the woman's gracefulness. And her hair, I really envied her hair. After my battle with the morning frizzies, I coveted its black, hip-hugging sleekness. Heck, I was even jealous of Tarzan's long, blond, meticulously-brushed tresses.

Jeez, what was wrong with me? I recalled the man's condescending attitude and flaunted muscles. How could I be jealous of someone so ridiculous? Yet I had to admit, he was awfully nice to Rosa when she came in for dinner the night before.

Rosa. The girl intrigued me. I wondered if I would get a chance to find out what thoughts danced behind those shy brown eyes. Somehow, she seemed to embody everything about Costa Rica I found so enchanting.

As I continued my march down the path, my mind worked its way around to the one person I had avoided thinking about. Lava-cake man. What was his story? Was he single?

Immediately, I squashed the idea. I didn't need that kind of complication. I had work to do, not to mention my dad sleeping in a bed not ten feet from my own.

Cozy.

I stumbled upon the spa. The thatched-roof structure snuggled into a clearing. Near the entrance, water splashed over a staircase of black volcanic rocks. The grounds shimmered with green. A mass of white orchids blanketed the area. It was the perfect look for a spa. Simple. Elegant.

I stopped. I didn't do elegant.

My editor had put me up to this. "Write about the spa," he'd said in that all-knowing way of his. "Women love spas." I was a woman. I was terrified of spas.

You have to get naked and let other people see your pouchy, less-than-perfect parts. Saunas are suffocating and the massage might hurt and what if? Oh no. I didn't shave my legs. I had been in such a rush this morning, I forgot.

That's gotta be bad.

The closest thing to a spa experience I had ever had was getting a *mani* and *pedi* with Kaylee. She'd had to talk me into it.

"For the love of Pete," she said. "Just because you think you're Adventure Girl doesn't mean you have to avoid encounters with nail polish." Kaylee was the sort of woman who thought it was a sin to wear open-toed shoes without polish.

I looked down at my feet. I had painted my toes for this

trip in Kaylee's honor. The peachy color was already chipping away.

I took a breath and marched to the front door of the spa.

I rapped on the door and wondered what kind of sin it was to have a massage without shaving my legs.

11

I think spas know they're scary.

So they try to hide it. Like when you go to the dentist and they play classical music to lull you while they prep the drill from hell. The dentist tries to make you feel warm and fuzzy by hanging pictures of cute and cuddly baby animals on the ceiling. Meanwhile, they berate your delicate teeth with gritty polish and squirt your sensitive gums with icy water.

Spas are better at hiding the scary stuff. The rooms are dim and they have fountains tinkling everywhere and fluty music floating around. The aroma of lavender and roses wafts about. All of this makes you forget that they are going to see that you don't workout, your body is imperfect, and you forgot to shave your legs.

"Bienvenidos." A woman with a soothing voice welcomed me at the door. "Please come with me."

I followed her inside. I watched her close the door with finality. There was no turning back.

"You are the writer?" She took my bag and placed it in a

lovely locker.

"Yes," I said. "Will it be all right if I take pictures of the spa?" I experienced a little separation anxiety as she locked away my camera.

"Of course. But no work now. You must relax." She picked up a cream-colored card with delicate lettering curving across the paper. "You are here for a half-day treatment. You have already selected from our menu. The chocolate hydrotherapy bath and cocoa butter massage."

"You're making me hungry."

The woman tucked the card into a file box. "We have a small cafe. Between treatments we invite you to select from our menu of crisp salads, healthy wraps, and refreshing smoothies."

Oh, I was kind of hoping for a menu of crisp cookies, unhealthy cakes, and refreshing milkshakes.

"We are happy to have you here," the woman said. "You write for a spa magazine, yes?"

"Well, actually, it's an adventure travel magazine."

"Oh. Well, I guess that is good, too."

Great. Not only is this place scary, but they were hoping I was someone else.

The woman led me into a chamber dimly lit by the flicker of candles. In the center, a whirlpool bath — just big enough for one person — hummed and burbled.

"Please," the woman curved her arm towards the bath. "Take your time undressing. You may enter the pool when you are ready. I will bring the chocolate essence aromatherapy." She left the shadowy room.

This was so weird.

I took off my clothes and placed a tentative toe in the swirling water. I was terrified that she might come back and find me buck naked, so I hurried to get in.

I swear she was spying on me, because the instant I got in the water, the woman returned. She added a few drops of the aromatherapy to the water. The scent of chocolate foamed through the ripples.

Wow. Maybe I could get used to this.

The woman lifted up my hair to keep the ends from trailing in the water. She tucked a pillow under my neck. "Now close your eyes and relax," she said. "Hydrotherapy is celebrated for its healing and restorative properties. Focus on the feather-light massage of the water. Allow it to calm your troubled emotions, ease the tension in your muscles, and lift your spirit." A faint swish indicated she had left the room.

I peeked open an eye to make sure, then I settled back. Okay now. What did she say? Focus. Warm water. Calm. Lift the spirit. Ease the tension of my muscles. Relax.

Oh crap. I have to pee.

Hold on now. It's only a half hour. You can make it. Think of something else.

There's just one problem with being forced to lie still, relax, and not think about peeing — it gives you a whole lot of time to think crappy things about yourself.

The upshot was this: I worked for an adventure magazine, I wrote adventure stories, and I stunk at adventuring. My dad's attire that morning had reminded me of a terrible fact. We were going white-water rafting.

And I was certain to louse it up.

The rotten thing was, I had wanted to be Adventure Girl since I toddled in diapers. My parents were still together back then and my mom would follow me around, plucking me from the tops of bookshelves and chiding me to keep my feet on the ground.

When I was a girl, I watched the boys whiz by our house on their bikes and I longed to discover what exhilarations they got into. So my parents bought me a hot-pink Huffy and for days I wobbled it around the road in front of our house until I got the hang of it. Then I ripped off the pink basket and the glittery mylar that fluttered from the handlebars. I rubbed the bike with mud so it looked less pink and begged to go with the boys. They had built a jump in the desert out of a mound of dirt and a few planks of wood. I watched their stunts and acrobatics with awe. My own attempt ended with my ass up in a mesquite bush.

Yet I persisted in viewing myself as a fearless adventurer. After my parents' divorce, my dad took me and a neighbor's son camping. I bashed through the woods exclaiming to the terrorized boy, "Have you ever seen a girl do this? What other girl would do that?"

I came to adulthood with a mind full of movies like *Star Wars* and *Terminator*, certain I was destined to become a kick-ass heroine like Princess Leia or Sara Connor.

But the designer of my gene code possessed a wicked sense of humor. "Let's give little Aurora an intense desire for adventure. Then we'll leave out her athleticism gene. Snicker, snicker."

Desire and practice only take you so far. Just as a great artist needs an eye for color, light, shade, and composition, a kick-ass female needs a knack for heroics. I, of course, had none. Thus, I was still a girl bashing about trying to impress everyone.

Well — ridiculous as I may be — I will never, EVER write for a spa magazine.

I survived the half hour. After a dash to the bathroom, the spa lady brought me to another room. The air inside cooled and soothed.

"Make your self comfortable," she said. "Lie face-down and rest your head here." She indicated a bed draped in creamy sheets. A horseshoe shaped pillow hovered at one end. "The masseuse will be here in a moment."

She discreetly left the room. I stripped down to my undies and crawled into the sheets. Heat emanated from the length of the bed. I told myself not to get too comfortable.

The masseuse arrived and covered me with a light cottony blanket. She deftly rolled the covers down to my waist, swept my hair away from the nape of my neck, and tucked a puffy pillow beneath my feet. She warmed cocoa oil between her palms and smoothed it down my back. She probed an array of pressure points along my spine. Her hands lifted. A hot towel unfurled over my skin. Warmth infused my tingling muscles.

Wait a minute. I wasn't actually liking this, was I?

The masseuse moved to my right leg, folded back the cover, skimmed warm oil down the length of my thigh and calf, then swirled her thumb in the space behind my knees. The tickle sent me into a fit of giggles.

What was happening to me?

The blanket lay over my leg again. A steamy washcloth wrapped around my foot. Fingers kneaded the heel, the arch, the ball. Warm oil smoothed over my skin.

Was I turning into a girlie-girl?

The towel and the blanket lifted. The woman asked me to roll over. She tucked the pillow under my knees and moved to my head, threading a hot rolled towel under my neck. She soothed hot oil down the length of my arm, massaged my wrist and the back of my hand, and pressed several points on my palm.

Great — next I would be wanting my bikini-line waxed, my eyebrows plucked, and my ears candled.

She glided oil over my collarbone, up the length of my neck, and across my shoulders. Her fingers slipped through my hair and massaged my scalp. She lifted my head and turned it to one side. Her fingers pressed to the base of my scalp. She turned my head the other way. Gently, she pressed again.

I was in serious trouble here.

She slid the warm cloth from beneath my neck and curled another steaming cloth around my face, laying it first on my chin, then across my cheekbones, and settling the ends over my eyes. I smelled the sharp scent of eucalyptus. Her hands slid underneath my head and pillowed it for some time, her fingertips dotting several pressure points.

Maybe I had it all wrong.

The cloth lifted from my eyes. A murmur told me she would leave me to dress. I lay still for a long time, completely unable to move. No longer was I a woman, but a puddle.

Maybe I should reconsider my career.

Maybe I should give up Adventure Girl.

Maybe I should become Spa Girl.

12

I managed to coagulate into a human being again.

I followed the smell of lunch to the lodge. The kitchen crew was busy setting out several steamy bowls. I saw Stacy curled up on a couch reading a book. I slid into the chair next to her. "Mind if I join you?" I asked.

She folded the corner of a page down and tossed the paperback aside. "I would love it. How was the spa?"

"Check this out. Their brochure says, *You will leave our spa in a state of sexy tranquility.*" I handed her the glossy card.

"Wow. Will you get a load of this place?" She held the card in her hands like it was a priceless document. "So do you?"

"What?"

"Feel sexy and tranquil?"

"Well, I don't know about the sexy part. But I feel more relaxed."

"I know what will help with the sexy." Stacy tipped her head towards the other side of the lodge. "Check it out."

Lava-cake man sat in a chair, also reading a book.

"I saw you scoping him out last night," Stacy said.

"Was I that obvious?"

"No, but I'm tuned in to these things. He looks like he's straight out of one of my romance novels."

"Oh?"

"Yeah." Stacy tapped the book beside her. "I'm kind of an addict. I've read hundreds. I want to write my own someday. You read romances?"

"I guess I'm more of a mystery buff."

"Yeah, well, hunky over there definitely has the tall-dark-handsome thing going on."

"I mostly see him as a big hunk of chocolate."

"Sweet and tasty. I like that. And by the way he wears that shirt, I'd say he's ripped, too."

"Ripped?"

"Oh yeah." Stacy fanned herself with her hand. "That's a favorite word in romances. The hero is always built, muscled, broad-shouldered, ripped."

"Sounds like he simply can't contain himself so he has to bust out of his shirt."

"Yeah, very Incredible Hulk. You should go talk to him."

"The Hulk's here?"

"No." Stacy said, exasperated. "Mr. Ripped of course."

"First there was Tarzan, now Mr. Ripped. I think you are going to be a novelist."

"You think so? Oh! Your last name is Night, right? That's perfect. We'll call it *Ripped Night.*"

"Well, if you put it that way." I stood up and sauntered across the lodge. I glanced back at Stacy and gave her a sly look.

She leaned over the back of her seat and watched the scene like a movie. The only thing she needed was a bag of popcorn.

I propelled myself towards lava-cake man.

Just before I reached him, I spun towards the food and picked up a plate. I peeked over my shoulder at Stacy. Her face crumpled. I shrugged, then reached for the spoon that was buried in the black beans and rice.

"Married."

I jumped at the smooth voice over my shoulder. I turned around and there he was — Mr. Ripped, aka Lava-cake man — smiling down at me with a plate in his hand. Did he just say something about marriage?

"Excuse me?"

"Casado." He pointed at the table. "Traditional Costa Rican cuisine. Black beans. Rice. Meat. Cabbage. Tomatoes. It's known as casado. The word translates as married, or more specifically, married man. It means the boring daily fare a man can expect to eat after he's been snagged into marriage."

"Nice."

"What can I say? These Ticos have a wicked sense of humor." He offered a hand. "I'm Anthony."

I accepted his hand. His fingers curled around mine, warm and strong. Anthony. Wait a minute. Is that like Antonio? "You don't happen to be a photographer, do you?"

"Kind of." He gestured towards his chair. A small camera bag perched on top of his book. "I mostly like to fool around."

I bet you do. "I, uh — I'm Aurora. It's a pleasure to meet you. What is it you do then? I mean, for a living?" Jeez, I sound like an idiot.

"I'm an archaeology professor at the University of— Are you all right?"

No. If there's one thing sexier than a photographer, it's definitely an archaeologist. Hmm. Indiana Jones. I could be the lost ark. "Yes, yes. Sorry. Where did you say you're from?"

"I didn't." He heaped beans, rice, and meat onto his plate. "I'm from California."

Like Californication.

Oh stop with the smutty mind already.

"You're a journalist." He added some sliced tomatoes to his plate.

Wow, you know something about me? "No. Yes. Sort of. I'm a staff writer for *See!*, a travel magazine." And I'm usually a lot more eloquent.

"That explains the heavy duty photography gear."

"Thank you — by the way — for bringing my camera bag to me this morning."

"No problem. You looked like you just woke up."

I blushed. Whatever gave you that idea? "That was kind of embarrassing."

"I wasn't embarrassed at all."

"You have a sense of humor, too."

"I have my moments." He spooned fried plantains into a small bowl. So he liked dessert. Definitely a point in his favor. "You on the other hand, Miss Aurora, were pretty em-bare-assed when I saw you." Definitely a point against.

I made a production out of selecting a napkin.

"Sorry. Couldn't resist." His expression was contrite. "So tell me, where are you from?"

"I'm American, too." I selected a knife and a fork.

"I see." His plate full, Anthony swiveled away from the table and looked me over from hair to sandal. "Pretty," he said after a while as though informing himself of an important decision. "But rude." He pivoted on his heel and strode back to his chair.

I stared after him with an empty plate in my hand. I couldn't believe it. Of all the nerve. How could he say such a thing? I didn't deserve that.

Did he really just call me pretty?

13

Rude? Rude!

That part just sank in.

What did I do? Look absent-mindedly at my watch? Say something? Not say something? Did I fail to make eye contact? I could be bad about that. Especially when I talked to someone who made me feel fluttery and nervous inside.

Or maybe it was just the opposite. Perhaps I stared. Or talked too much. Or didn't shake his hand right.

Jeez, I just got here yesterday. The man could cut me some slack.

Whatever it was, it must have been pretty bad for him to comment on it. I mean, he actually said I was rude.

Who does that?

I was on my way to the village, walking beside my dad, a little ways behind the rest of the tour group. My dad didn't notice my torment.

The mile from the lodge to the village wasn't nearly so bad without the burden of our luggage and the tirade of the monsoon storm. We were on our way to the village to observe the programs the lodge sponsored in the local community.

It was the perfect opportunity for me to start my article. I was prepared. I had a notebook filled with clean, bright pages just waiting to absorb details of the setting, jewels of information about the culture, and poignant quotes from the locals. My camera swung at my side, loaded with an empty twenty-gigabyte card, freshly charged batteries, and my best zoom lens.

I was ready.

Except all I could think of was Anthony. Where was he? And why in the world did he say I was rude?

I didn't realize we had made it to the village until the group stopped in front of a little elementary school, a bright blue building with a few classrooms that opened onto a covered veranda.

A teacher greeted us. She crowded us into one of the classrooms. A dozen students sat at desks, each neatly dressed in a white and blue uniform. The children took turns standing up to introduce themselves.

A familiar girl leaped up. "Me llamo Rosa." She plopped back down in her chair, propped an elbow on her desk, and watched the boy next to her as he made his introduction. I had already requested permission to take photos in the school, so I lifted my camera and framed a shot.

Rosa giggled and blushed as the boy next to her said his name. I wondered if she had a crush on him. Through the zoomed lens I saw sprigs of Rosa's hair pulling free from her ponytail. A pink plastic barrette tucked her bangs away from her face. A few stray wisps curled in the humid air.

I had barely clicked off a couple of shots when the teacher herded us out of the room and onto the veranda. There, a group of older students formed a ring around the covered patio. They stood in pairs, ready to dance. The boys sported straw cowboy hats, crisp white shirts, and red bolo ties. The girls wore long skirts; they held them up like the wings of butterflies.

The younger children streamed out of the classroom to watch. Rosa perched on the edge of a chair and swung her feet in anticipation.

A Latin beat poured out of a boom box tucked onto a window ledge. The circle of dancers began to spin, the girls swirling their skirts around their feet, the boys skipping and bowing and dipping to the beat.

I used a wide angle lens to draw in the entire whirling spiral. I slowed down the shutter speed to capture an image of streaking color. The girls' fast-moving skirts created washes of yellow, orange, and red.

Through the lens, I spied Anthony.

He was on the other side of the dancers, watching me.

The pinwheel of dancers picked up speed. Then they flew apart. A small hand grasped mine. A boy tugged me towards the center of the veranda.

I looked up just as Rosa took Anthony's hand.

I couldn't help but watch the two of them as they started to dance. Anthony pretended he couldn't get the steps right. He made silly kicks and false stumbles while keeping them spinning in perfect time.

Rosa was delighted. She scolded and chided and preached at him for his ineptitude. Anthony leaned over and said something to her that elicited a peal of giggles. Rosa chastened him some more and Anthony slid into a perfect execution of the steps.

Rosa beamed triumphantly, exuding the satisfaction of a superior dancer and gifted teacher all rolled into one.

Anthony's eyes locked on mine.

My cheeks flushed and I turned back to my own partner, who wasn't having as much fun as Rosa, poor kid.

Stuck with me.

Then Anthony was beside me. He took my hand away from the boy, who scurried off with a look of relief. Anthony swung me around the circle at a fast — yet graceful — pace.

Clearly, his bad dancing had only been an act. I admired the way he'd drawn Rosa out of her shyness.

I had little time to think as I tried to keep up. But one question did manage to float up in my mind. Why was Anthony dancing with me when two hours before he'd called me rude?

The music wound down. I noticed Rosa watching us balefully.

"Anthony," I said. "While I'm sure my partner is grateful that you cut in, I don't think yours is too happy."

He gave me a devastating bow and skipped back over to Rosa. The girl's face lit like a sparkler as he swept her into the last dance.

As the song's final notes churned out of the boom box, I gathered up my notebook and camera gear. By the time I looked around again, Anthony was nowhere to be seen.

Our guide, Luis, met us after the performance. He led us to the local *pulperia* — a combination soda shop and corner store — in the center of town. "You like the dancing?" he asked.

Everyone, including the typically dour newlyweds, beamed at him with flushed and cheerful faces.

"The children thrive when they start doing the dances," Luis said. "It lights them up. They grow their personality. It gives them a self esteem."

Oh! Here it was. The kind of material I needed for my article. Of course, I wasn't writing it down. I scrabbled around for my notebook.

"We have much pride in education in Costa Rica," Luis continued. "Our children, they learn English better than we do. In school, they study art, music, math, social studies, science, even the environment."

Where the heck was my pen?

"Our government is good. Gives us free education, free healthcare, many social services."

I must have put it in my camera bag.

"Our country affords this because it has no army."

Aha! Here it is. I poised the pen above my notebook.

Luis turned away. He was done talking.

I lowered my pen in defeat.

The lady who ran the *pulperia* leaned out of a window — the kind you find at a walk-up ice cream shop — and handed Luis several cups of a cold, creamy drink.

Luis passed them around. "A *refresco*." He told us the thick, smoothie-like concoction was a local favorite. A blend made of rice and cola and a tomato-like fruit.

"Now wait just a minute, Luis," one of the college boys said. "You said you have no army, but you must have an air force, right?"

"No," Luis handed him the pulpy drink. "No military."

"That can't be right," the kid said. "In *Jurassic Park*, the Costa Rican Air Force obliterated the island with the dinosaurs. Are you saying that was all made up?"

On the trek back to the lodge, Luis's words sunk in.

Costa Rica had no military. I could only imagine what my veteran father thought of that.

When I reached the room, I dug out my guidebook. Sure enough, in 1949, Costa Rica's president, Don Pepe Figueres, smashed the wall of a military fortress with a sledgehammer, then he nonchalantly handed the keys to the fortress over to the minister of public education and told him to make it into a museum.

The country had not had an army since.

It fascinated me that Central America was stereotyped as a backwards place locked in civil war, corruption, and violence. For there I was, experiencing another side — a graceful side — that most of the world never saw. Walking among the people in the village, I felt the strength of their national and cultural pride, their intelligence and education, and their friendly and welcoming attitude towards visitors.

I had found a place with no army.

A place with no war.

That evening, as I made my way over to the lodge, an unusually peaceful feeling settled over me. I even paused to admire Tico-the-gator lounging in his pond.

But when I reached the lodge, the peace evaporated.

14

I tried to duck out of sight, but it was too late.

Inside the lodge, over by the kitchen, mounding food on his plate, stood my tormentor. Anthony. His dish overflowed with speckled *gallo pinto*, crispy fried fish, fluffy corn tortillas, and juicy ripe pineapple.

It was too late to hide. He had already seen me.

I stalked to the opposite end of the buffet table, moving in a wide arc around him.

The man had called me rude. I was not going to speak to him, not going to let him know it bothered me, not going to create a fuss. I was going to mind my own business, keep my cool, be aloof, stay calm, stay collected, stay dignified.

Anthony wheeled away from his end of the buffet table. He strode straight towards me. Then he dazzled me with a crooked smile.

I raised my nose high. "Why'd you call me rude?" I blurted. Damn.

Anthony plucked a chunk of pineapple from his plate and popped it in his mouth.

I tried to be mad at him, but the fact was, being in such close proximity to him made me feel a lot of things. None of them was anger.

The emotions on my face must have been obvious. Anthony's eyes danced with amusement.

"Well?" I demanded.

"You said you're American."

"Yeah. So?"

"Think about where you are." He sidestepped me and swung into a chair at one of the smaller tables. Just big enough for two. He wanted me to follow him.

I couldn't. I wouldn't.

I rushed through the line and slopped food onto my plate. Then I whirled in defiance. Stacy sat by herself at a table at the far end of the lodge, reading a book. I should go sit with her.

I looked from Stacy to Anthony. He was shoveling black beans and rice into his face and pretending I didn't exist.

Definitely Stacy.

I took a step towards her. She seemed engrossed in her book. Maybe I shouldn't bother her. I slid my gaze back over to Anthony. Probably I shouldn't leave things unresolved with him. A kick-ass heroine would face up to confrontation. Not back down from it.

I marched over and plunked my plate down on Anthony's table. "Are you going to give me a straight answer?"

"Like I said — think about it. Where are you?"

"A lodge? The jungle? Costa Rica?"

"Think bigger."

"Central America."

"Bingo."

I didn't like his haughty tone. "So what's your point?"

"You can't come to Central America and tell people you're American."

"What's the big deal?"

"It's rude."

"So you've said."

"Eat your dinner. Then I'll show you something."

Bossy.

I did as I was told. Anthony didn't look up from his plate. We ate our dinners in silence.

"Come on." He picked up our empty dishes. They clattered as he dropped them on a table that had been set out to collect them.

He placed a hand lightly on my back. We wove through the scatter of tables to the opposite side of the lodge. We stopped in front of a map that papered the wall. Pins with red, yellow, and blue tops stuck out of the map. Most were clustered in Europe. They indicated where the lodge's visitors came from.

Anthony handed me a red pin. "Here. Stick this in your home town."

I pushed the pin into a spot in the lower part of New Mexico. "Aren't you going to put one in?" I asked.

"Already did."

"You going to give me a geography lesson, or what?"

"Just look. There's the Americas. North, Central, and

South. People from the U.S., we think we have a monopoly on the word American."

A breeze fluttered through the lodge. It caught a whiff of soap — or maybe it was shampoo or shaving cream — off Anthony and carried it my way. Whatever it was, the heady scent was intensified by the heat and humidity.

"So," he said. "It's rude to tell people 'I'm American' like we're somehow entitled."

"But our country is called America."

"No. It's the United States of America. It's like someone from Germany telling someone from Italy, *I'm European.*"

"I get your point. You still didn't have to call me rude."

"It was my way of pulling your pigtails."

Wait — what?

"Did you know Christopher Columbus didn't even land in the U.S.?" Anthony asked.

"No. Maybe. So?"

"He came to the Americas four different times and landed here, here, and here." He pointed to the Bahamas and Central and South America.

I stepped closer to the map for a better look. Anthony moved directly behind me. He was so close, I could feel him, though we didn't touch.

"Of course," he said. "It's not your fault."

"Now something's my fault?"

"Sure. We northerners naturally have a stretched ego. It comes from using maps like this our whole lives."

"First I'm rude, then I'm at fault, now I have a big ego? Where does it end?"

Anthony leaned in to point at the map again. His shoulder brushed against mine. "See up here? At the top? When the round earth was flattened to make this map, it had to be stretched to make it fit into a rectangle."

I could feel him lean away again.

"The continents in the north are stretched. That sends us a subliminal message. We're bigger and better than the south."

"Come on," I said. "People don't really think that."

"Maybe not consciously. But look. Greenland is bigger than South America on this map. It's actually eight or nine times smaller."

"Really? South America's that big?"

"See what I mean?"

How could I resist a man who found importance in such things? I snuck a peek at him. His closeness startled me.

Anthony bent his head nearer.

My dad came out of nowhere.

"I always like to think of the Americas as a woman," he said, pushing between us. "Buxom North America, hippy, long-legged South America, and skinny-waisted Central America. My kind of woman."

"For crying out loud, Dad. It doesn't look anything like a woman. There's not even a face."

"Face? Who said anything about a face?"

I rolled my eyes. My dad winked at Anthony who smiled back with that infuriating all-knowing look that men have.

"You two enjoy your continental pin-up girl. I'll see you around." I started to exit the lodge.

The newlywed couple nearly knocked me over in their haste to bound up the front steps.

"What's going on?" I asked.

"Luis's daughter," they both panted. "She's gone."

15

Anthony, Stacy, and my dad were beside me in an instant.

The newlyweds had run all the way from the village. The heat and humidity were oppressive. We brought over chairs and encouraged the couple to sit down.

I fetched two glasses of water.

"Tell us what happened," I said.

The wife gulped the water. "We don't know. There's a big commotion down in the village. Apparently, Rosa never came home from school. Everyone is searching for her."

One of the cooks emerged from the kitchen. She overheard our conversation. "Come with me," she said. "I will drive you."

We ran outside and climbed into a rusted-out van parked behind the lodge. The vehicle jumped and jarred as we flew down the road to the village.

When we got out of the van, people swarmed around us in confusion. Most of them were congregating around a wood-paneled house that drooped at the end of the road.

We moved down the street and stopped several feet from the front door. Luis held a woman in his arms. The woman held an infant in hers. They examined a piece of paper held by a man we had not met. We did not want to interfere, so we stood silent and still, too.

Luis noticed us. He took the sheet of paper from the young man, said a few words to him, and pointed in our direction. The man drifted over to us.

"My name is Hector," he said. "I am Luis's nephew. He

asked me to make sure you are taken care of." He lifted his hands and ushered us farther back. "Since you are here, I assume you know about Luis's daughter."

"What happened to her?" Anthony asked.

"Someone took her."

"Who would do such a thing?" my father asked.

"We don't know."

"Maybe she just got lost," I said.

"No." Hector glanced back at Luis. "You will find out anyway I am sure. A note was left. The person who took her wants money."

"Oh my god," Stacy said.

"You must excuse me," Hector said. "I will help Luis. Please go back to the lodge. I am to take Luis's place as your guide. First, I must see what I can do."

The rest of the group made their way to the van. I was rooted to the spot, lost in dark thoughts, overcome by the realization that while the nation of Costa Rica had eschewed war for more than half a century, it's a basic fact of human existence that where there are people, there is conflict. Here in this peaceful village, on this beautiful day, someone had done the unthinkable. Taken Rosa and declared war on her and her family.

I looked at the faces of the villagers. All around me, they stood in shocked and grieved silence. My dad placed a hand at my elbow. Wordlessly, he guided me back to the van. I folded into a seat and thought of the woven grasshopper beside my bed.

"You can't do anything," my dad insisted.

"Why not?" I paced in the lodge. My father and Anthony watched me.

"It's not your responsibility," my dad said.

"But—"

"Your dad's right." Anthony was sitting on a chair, leaning forward, elbows on his knees, hands clasped together. "It's too dangerous."

"But I can't sit here and do nothing." I said, a frantic edge in my voice. "We've got to find her."

"You're not the police," Anthony said. "You're just a writer."

"Just a writer?" My voice became a little high-pitched and squeaky.

"Calm down." Anthony got up. "I mean that you're not trained in this kind of thing. Leave it to the professionals."

"I don't even think the village has any police."

"They'll bring someone in." Anthony tried to coax me into the chair he'd abandoned.

"I don't want to sit down," I snapped. "Dad, won't you help me?"

"Help you what?" he asked. "Who do you think you are? Some sort of super-sleuth?"

My face flamed red.

"You've been reading too many of those mystery novels with that park ranger, what's-her-name?"

"Anna Pigeon." Another kick-ass female. Damn her.

"You're not in law enforcement," my dad said. "You don't carry a gun. You don't even know any self defense."

"I know," I said, my voice small.

My dad let up. "Look, sweetie. I know you're worried about the girl, but she'll be found."

I stopped pacing and scritched the toe of my shoe across the hard wood floor.

"Besides," my dad continued. "You have a job to do."

I thought of the empty pages filling up my notebooks. I didn't say anything.

"It's getting late," my dad said. "I'm going to the room. Will you come with me?"

"I'll stay here for a while."

My dad looked uncertainly at Anthony. Then he stomped out into the night.

Anthony waited to speak until my dad was gone. "I know you don't know me very well, but is it all right if I give you a hug?"

The lodge grew hazy as I focused on Anthony. I liked the way his dark features set off the light in his eyes. "Sure." I crossed my arms in front of me. "I guess so."

He hugged me. Not one of those hugs where someone raises an arm and gives you a half-hearted pat on the back. A hug that wrapped so tightly around my shoulders, Anthony could have patted his own back. I think it might have been a bit too tight. When he let go, I felt a little squishy inside.

"Come on," he said. "Let's get a drink."

I followed him to the bar. We deposited ourselves on a pair of twisty stools. Anthony ordered a beer and a glass of wine.

When the drinks arrived, he picked up the beer — droplets of water were already condensing on the cold glass — and took a slow sip.

"Do you remember what I told you?" he asked.

"About what?"

"Columbus."

"You're changing the subject."

"Humor me," he said.

"Of course." I remembered everything he'd said. And most of what he hadn't, too.

"He landed in Costa Rica."

"And?"

"Called it the Rich Coast."

"You're trying to distract me," I said.

"Is it working?"

"No."

"Liar."

"You're calling me names again."

"If the shoe fits—"

"Shut up. Distract me," I said sourly. "I'm not allowed to do anything anyway."

"Try to control the undying gratitude."

I shot him an irritated look.

"It was because of the gold."

"What?"

"Keep up," he said.

"Excuse me for worrying about Rosa."

"Columbus saw gold."

"Fine, I give. Where did he see gold?"

"The natives wore it."

"Necklaces? Bracelets?"

"Sure — ornaments, headbands, that sort of thing."

"Bad news for the natives," I said.

"The conquistadors took it all."

"Greedy bastards."

"You know the story."

"Murder, disease, slavery. The downfall of a proud people."

"Precisely." Anthony slid the base of his glass around in the ring of dew it had left on the bar.

"Are there any artifacts left?" I asked.

"In museums. It's likely there's more out there, but it's

difficult to get permission for new digs."

"So that's why you're here, isn't it?" I asked. "To study the history."

Anthony rested his arm on the bar and leaned closer. "You like mysteries, right?" His voice was conspiratorial.

"Sure."

"Costa Rica has one that's every bit as mysterious as Stonehenge."

I was skeptical. "I've never heard of it."

"Of course not," he said. "There's a bit of a marketing problem."

"You're going to make me work for this, aren't you?"

"Spheres," he said. "Hundreds of mysterious granite spheres. Perfectly round to within a centimeter. They've been found all over this region. Nobody knows their origin."

"Is that so?"

"You don't believe me." Anthony moved back. "They exist. Some are tiny, the size of an orange." He cupped his hands around an imaginary piece of fruit. "Others are six feet tall — my height — and weigh as much as sixteen tons."

"So where are they?"

"The spheres have been found along river banks and in cemeteries." Anthony drained his beer. "No one knows how they were made. Or how they were shaped so perfectly round. They rival the precision of the stones used to build the pyramids in Egypt."

"And how exactly did they move sixteen tons of granite to a cemetery?"

"Don't know. Some were found miles from the source."

"And I suppose no one knows what they mean, either?"

"Nope. The people who made them were probably long gone even before the Spanish arrived."

"Aren't the stones still here?" I asked. "You haven't told me why I've never heard of these spheres."

"Like I said, marketing."

"You are going to make me work for this."

"Some are still in their original locations. Some made it into the National Museum. But most were plundered long ago and used to decorate the gardens of expensive homes."

"And?"

Anthony's eyes gleamed. "Marketing?"

"You're as impossible as my dad."

"Okay, okay, here it is. Europe has Stonehenge, Egypt the Great Pyramids, and Costa Rica—"

I leaned closer.

"Costa Rica," Anthony said, "has big balls."

I flushed and moved away. "Ah, leave it to a man."

"Excuse me?"

"I see your point. With minds like yours, marketing would be a problem."

"Seriously, though. You should check out the spheres sometime. They're quite beautiful."

I lifted my wine and took a drink. Through the bottom of the glass, I saw Anthony watching me.

"Like you," he said.

I sputtered wine all over the front of my shirt.

Anthony handed me a napkin, but when I closed my fingers around it, he took my hand. He leaned in.

I closed my eyes and held my breath.

I toppled off the stool.

16

I lay on the floor, flat on my back, and concentrated on Anthony's face.

"Aurora?" he said. "Are you all right?"

What the hell happened? How could I have fallen? A different face loomed into view. My father. He's what happened. I didn't fall. I remembered now. There had been a tug at my sleeve just before I fell. My dad pulled me off that stool. I was leaning forward. Anthony was about to kiss me. My dad yanked me away.

I ignored the hands that reached out to help. I grabbed the base of the stool and hoisted myself up. My cheeks flared and my eyes burned, whether it was from anger or embarrassment, I couldn't be sure.

"I'm sorry Anthony," I said. I fled from the lodge.

Tico was out of the water, lounging in the dark by the side of the trail.

"You better get out of my way," I said.

Tico slithered into the water and glared at me.

"You look like I feel," I told him. I stomped up the path towards the bungalow. When I reached the room I grabbed my daypack and crammed things inside. I was punching the strap of my camera into the bag when my dad came in.

"Aurora—"

"What? What do you want?"

"I didn't mean to—"

"You did."

It's a cruel joke, the way people are programmed with

offset timers and discordant response systems. A person hoping for a hug gets only indifference. An expectation of praise yields a mere nod of approval. A partner is sad while the other is joyful, a child is bored and a sibling content. When one longs for quiet, a friend wants noise. A person reading is disturbed by a neighbor talking. A sympathetic ear comes a moment too late. A stranger looking for love comes a day too soon. One person's clouds obscure another's sun.

At that moment, standing there in the room between the two twin beds, my father and I were terribly out-of-sync.

"Where are you going?" he asked.

"It's none of your business."

"I don't like him."

"Of course you don't," I said, "he's a man and not you."

"I'm a father," he said. "Sue me."

Above our heads, the ceiling fan pushed the blades around, trying to move the still air. I pushed my emotions around with similar effort, trying to still my spinning thoughts. My dad looked from me to the fan, perhaps hoping it would reveal a clue on how to deal with a pain-in-the-ass daughter.

"You shouldn't be here," I said.

"You're angry."

"What astounding powers of observation you have."

"You're angry because I took the job."

"My job."

I had celebrated with Kaylee when I got the job with *See!* We hiked up a mountain with two bottles of wine and a box of cheese nips. We found an overlook with two rocks just right for sitting, got drunk, and spent the night singing *Pour Some Sugar on Me* and giggling at the stars that spangled about and refused to stay in their proper places.

"Why didn't you tell me?" my dad asked.

"Because of this," I said.

"This what?"

"Your hurt feelings."

I could see it, too. The hurt in his eyes, though he would die a thousand deaths before he would admit it.

"You're the one that entered it," he said.

I had found the story in my dad's files. The pages had yellowed behind the typed black letters. I started reading it before I knew what it was. Then I couldn't stop. He had written a story about the war and about death and about triumph. As I read it, I knew I was seeing a deep part of him he had kept hidden away like an heirloom in a safe. Later, I found out about the contest and asked him to submit the story.

"You refused to enter it," I said. "So I did."

"I hate contests."

"You always wanted to go back to Vietnam."

That was one thing about my father I could never comprehend. Why he wanted to be reminded of the war that created the long black wall that slithers like a serpent through the National Mall. This was something I simply could not fathom.

"You went to Vietnam, too," he said.

"Because Nelle wouldn't leave the dogs."

"You hated it."

No. But I would die a thousand deaths before I would admit it.

"So what's the problem?" he asked.

"My editor." All of this was his fault, really. He insisted we write an article together about our trip to Vietnam.

"It was a good story," my dad said.

"He gave you my job." My dad was supposed to live in his world.

"That pisses you off."

I was supposed to live in mine. "Another brilliant deduction."

I wanted more than anything to deduce my way out of the room right then. I tried to figure out if I had forgotten anything.

"Why does it piss you off so much?" my dad asked.

"You're Sherlock. Figure it out." I found a notebook and pen and added them to the overstuffed bag.

"Come on," my dad said. "Tell me."

"Seven." I cast about for anything else I might need.

"Seven what?"

"Years."

The endless nights writing, the weekends of mailing queries, revising drafts, polishing manuscripts, collecting rejection slips, all in the vague hope I might someday land my dream job.

"It takes time," my dad said.

"Not for you."

"I see."

"One story," I said. "Same job."

"I wasn't trying to—"

"You did."

We regarded each other for a moment. The only sound was the whuff-whuff-whuff of the ceiling fan as it sluggishly churned the humid air.

"I worry about you," my dad said.

"I'm almost thirty," I said, "in case you hadn't noticed."

"At least if I'm with you I—"

"Can what, Dad?"

"Protect you."

"By pushing me off stools?" The memory of the interruption in the lodge brought another bubble of anger.

"I love you," my dad said.

"Believe me," I said, "you've made that clear."

"What's that supposed to mean?"

"Nothing."

"Fine."

"I'm going now." I gave up trying to figure out if I had everything I needed. I hoisted the bag to my shoulder, it felt heavy.

"Tell me," my dad said.

"It's a stupid memory," I said. "That's all."

"The divorce?"

"I remember the airport." Those were the days when family and friends could still accompany you to the gate. They could go through security and wait with you for your flight until the very second you boarded the plane.

"What about the airport?" my dad asked.

"I turned." My parents were splitting up. I assumed it was my fault.

"You looked back?"

"Yes." My mom had just handed the lady at the door our tickets. I broke away and ran to look back at my dad. I didn't want to go. I didn't want to leave my daddy behind.

"I didn't know," he said.

"Well, I do. And I saw you." I moved over to the door and curled my fingers around the handle. Unable to look him in the eyes, I stared down at the door handle in my hand. "You cried," I said.

The tears on my dad's cheek had looked foreign. He

had shoved his hands in his pockets and shuffled away, his head down, his back hunched. I had never seen him that way before. I had never seen him that way since.

"You're not still leaving?" my dad asked.

"I'm still mad."

"Where will you go?"

"I have a place."

"You hardly know him."

I twisted the latch and pulled the door open. "Yes, Dad," I said. "Thanks to you." I left, letting him think I was going to stay the night with Anthony. I actually planned to stay with Tico. In the lodge by his pool.

When I got there, I found a couch with a pillow. It started to rain. The palm leaf roof absorbed the sound. Outside, the rain pattered on the pond, on the jungle, and on the gravel path. But inside the lodge, it was quiet.

I didn't have a sheet or a blanket so I lay on the couch and curled up beneath my guilt.

17

That night the dream returned.

It flickered across the blank wall of my mind like an old projector spinning out grainy reels of badly spliced images. Even as it started flashing, I knew.

I knew that we were too late.

Through the door. Someone pushed me.

Dim. The room around. Gaping. Empty cots. That one

overturned. Spilling despair. Where the men — Stench. Bodies unwashed. Bedding filthy. Latrines unemptied. Tasted it. Crawling down my throat. Turning away. Hand grabbing my shoulder. Pointing. Over there. Twisted. What—?

A cage. Inside. Shadow. Curled. Her?

God, no. Rosa.

The heavy dark air of the lodge rushed down. It crushed me into the couch where I slept. I tried to breathe. Choked on the humidity. Rolled to the side, slung my feet to the floor, leaned over.

My hair falling forward. My breath won't come. The dream.

I hadn't had the dream since the months after Kaylee—

A rustle.

I jolted into full awareness. My head snapped up. My lungs sucked in air. Listened.

Nothing. The breeze. Perhaps an animal.

I hurled my gaze at the pond. Moonlight glinted on water. Two staring eyes glowed. Tico. Must have twitched his tail or inched through the undergrowth.

"I got you!" A voice from the dark.

Left me raw, clawing my way back into the comfort of my skin. Instinctively, I retreated into the inky black shadow formed by the cushions on the couch. I tucked my knees under my chin and grasped the soles of my bare feet. Listened.

Silence.

Was I awake? Hearing things? Why was I out here? My mind swirled in confusion. What the hell was going on?

"You still there?"

I closed my eyes. Tried to disappear.

"Hello?"

Trembled. Opened my eyes. The only light a sickly green glow from a digital clock. A shadow blocking it. A rasping sound at the bar.

"Christ the service here is lousy. I been trying to get you for— What? Yes!"

Opened my eyes. Service? Slow down. Breathe. Arrange your thoughts into something coherent. Concentrate. The rasping sound was the refrigerator, opening, closing. And the voice. Someone on the phone. Yes, that's it. But who?

"You'll get what you paid for!" The person. Familiar.

Tarzan.

Get a grip. Probably doesn't even know you're here.

As if in confirmation, the phone's receiver slammed into the cradle, a beer popped and fizzed, and shoes flip-flopped out of the lodge.

Minutes dripped by.

I didn't look around. I didn't crawl from the fold of the couch. I didn't move at all. I lay curled in defense, prepared to fight off any demons that appeared in my dreams or any devils that manifested in the lodge. I shut my eyes to the whole world. Closed my mind to all thought.

Fear ebbed out. Exhaustion flowed in.

Sleep overcame.

"Aurora?"

I jerked awake. Stacy stared down at me. The morning sun brushed her hair gold. After the night I had, she looked like an angel.

"You okay?"

The mind plays strange tricks with dreams. Piecing together a memory that is not mine of things that passed long ago, weaving in a person from my present that I barely know, and creating a reality that does not exist. I do not believe in foresight and premonitions, only in minds that tumble about in sleep, playing mean tricks and wreaking havoc on the psyche, leaving the sleeper in turmoil when she wakes.

I pushed myself up.

Stacy perched on the chair across from me. "Rough night?"

"I had a bad dream."

"Is that all?"

I held my head in my hands. I couldn't rid myself of the weight pressing on me and the gloom fogging up my mind. I realized Stacy was expecting an answer. "Someone used the phone in the night," I said.

"I don't mean to pry. But why are you out here?"

"My dad. We had a fight."

"Anthony?" The girl was uncanny in her perceptiveness.

"Silly, huh? You'd think I was in high school."

"You can stay with me." Stacy said. "I have an extra bed."

"How'd that happen?"

"You think I'd room with one of those slobs?" Stacy leaned back and threw her leg over the arm of the chair. "We paid for double occupancy, but they're all sharing the room next to me. The lodge lent them a fold-up bed."

"They don't mind?"

"They're guys."

The fog of sleep and dreams slid away as we talked. Sharp points of sunlight jabbed me fully awake. "You didn't bring a friend?" I asked. "A girl?"

"I tried. When they found out I wasn't going to the

beach, they weren't interested. The guys were easy. The rafting and all that."

"I admit, I was surprised—"

"To find a ditzy blonde here?"

"That's not what I—"

"Just kidding. You're right. I mean, I guess I don't seem the type. You really want to know?"

"Tell me," I said. "Or I'll feed you to Tico."

Stacy flashed a braces-straight, white-strip smile. "My dad's a doctor. So I grew up with money. My friends, too. In junior high, we'd hang out at this park in our neighborhood. We figured we were too old for the playground stuff, but we'd stand on the swings and sit on top of the equipment where you weren't supposed to be and talk about boys."

"Can't go wrong with boys."

"Sometimes this other girl would come. She was younger and still liked to go down the slides and stuff. I think her mom brought her because the parks in their neighborhood weren't nice. Anyway, one time my friends made fun of her and I was too much of a wimp to stop them. The girl never came back. Since then, I've always felt kind of, you know, apart."

I did know.

"Last semester I took this class. The professor, well, I guess he didn't like to teach, or something. He'd bring in this old-fashioned slide projector and all these stacks of slide trays. Then he'd spend the whole class showing us pictures of all these cool places. It bored the other kids, but I loved it."

So there was something more to Stacy then lime-green gum and romance novels.

"Then one day," she said, "I asked my teacher how he got

all those pictures. He said, *I went places*. I told him I'd been places, but I'd never seen anything like what he showed us. He asked where I'd been. I told him. He was like, *Young lady, going to resorts isn't going places.* The next day he gave me some brochures. One was for Piedras Blancas Lodge. It had a picture of the kids from the school. I guess they reminded me of the girl from the playground."

"So what did you think?" I asked.

"Of?"

"The school?"

"Oh, I don't know," Stacy said. "The kids seem happy."

"But?"

"Well, I mean, I wonder if they like doing that or if they feel kind of forced. I guess it gets them out of class for a while."

"You should ask them."

"What? Talk to them?"

"I saw a playground in the village."

Stacy's eyes lit with understanding.

I moved into her room.

18

What else would this trip bring?

Our group gathered in the lodge. I kept my distance from my dad. He had arrived first, along with the newlyweds. I came in with Stacy. Her three guy friends dragged in last. I hadn't seen Anthony, but he wasn't actually part of our group.

The eight of us milled about uncertainly. We had a tour scheduled for nine a.m., but we didn't know what was going on with our guides. We didn't know what was going on with Rosa.

Hector arrived right on time. Today I noticed that he was hardly more than a boy, perhaps the same age as the college kids. Except he didn't have the soft drinking bellies sported by his peers from the north. Instead, he had the wiry look of a man accustomed to hard work.

Stacy asked the question we were all thinking, "Have they found Rosa?"

"Not yet," Hector said. "Luis is working on it." That was obviously all we were going to get. Hector steered us outside. He set off at a clip down the road towards the village.

I trailed behind the group, avoiding my dad and longing to do something that would help Rosa. I wanted to be like the characters in movies and books. They always had solutions. They always knew what to do. Princess Leia and Sarah Connor and Anna Pigeon never lazed around getting massages, obsessing over chocolate, and mooning over men. They didn't procrastinate. They acted. They saved the day. They kicked ass.

Why did I have to be so pathetic?

Hector led us to a fenced-in area.

Within the enclosure, leaves blanketed the ground. A few plants scraggled in one corner. Hollowed out logs crisscrossed like a network of tiny bridges. Nothing moved.

We gathered around Hector.

"Profits from the lodge," he said, "help sponsor our paca breeding program." He closed and latched the gate. Then he looped his way around to one of the scooped-out logs. He made a hissing noise and tapped on the log with his foot. Nothing happened.

Hector moved around the enclosure, hissing and tapping until a set of long whiskers and two beady eyes poked out of the end of one of the logs. Soon, five piglet-sized animals scurried around, keeping their distance from us and looking annoyed.

"Hey," Stacy said. "That's the animal Rosa was holding."

"This is the agouti paca," Hector said. "This animal is endangered because of hunting."

"Who would hunt an oversized rat?" my dad asked.

"The meat is very good," Hector said.

"Ewww," Stacy said. "People eat rodents?"

"You would, too," Hector said, "if you could not buy shrink-wrapped meat at the market."

"Oh." Stacy bowed her head.

"Actually," Hector said, "paca meat is valuable. Hunters get ten dollars per kilo for the meat. If they hunt twice a week, with two animals they make the salary of a month."

"Will you reintroduce these to the wild?" I asked.

"The three with the tags in their ears are breeding pairs. Unfortunately, two of them escaped the other day. We recovered the female, but the male is still missing."

So that's why Rosa was in the middle of the road. She was chasing the fugitives.

"Their offspring," Hector said, "we donate to other breeding projects or introduce into the wild. We do not handle the young. They must fear humans if they are to avoid the hunters."

As we talked, the beady-eyed critters snuck back into their houses. We had disturbed their sleep.

"Luis used to hunt the paca," Hector continued. "Now he uses his knowledge of the animal to run the breeding program. The lodge gives him work, so he does not need to hunt."

I couldn't help but admire a man who opted for a long work week over quick money. I felt a flash of anger at the person who could commit such an atrocity against a good man.

We left the pacas alone and trudged back to the lodge through thick, humid air. My camera hung uselessly at my side. I had been so preoccupied with thoughts of Rosa that I had forgotten to take pictures of the strange little animals.

"Lunch today will be at eleven," Hector said when we'd reached the lodge's front steps. "I will meet you back here at noon for the afternoon tours." He left. Our group filed into the lodge and scattered.

After trekking through the heat and humidity, I needed a drink. Something cold and sweet. I sat down at the bar. Grace brought me a dewy glass of iced lemonade. The chilly drink flooded through me, rejuvenating my body.

But my spirit drooped.

Hector had made it clear that Rosa's disappearance was not any of our concern. We were only tourists after all, outsiders. Yet why did I feel so involved? I studied the couch where I had slept. Now instead of inky blackness pooling there, sunlight splayed across the cheery red cushions. Tarzan had been right over here at the bar.

He'd been so close.

I looked around for the phone. It sat askew on a pile of books, as though it might not have been touched since Tarzan slammed it down.

I sipped my lemonade and scoffed at myself.

What was I going to do? Call in CSI to dust for prints on the phone? Or the ransom note? Heck — I didn't even know if you could lift prints off paper. My dad and Anthony were right. I didn't know anything about forensics or law enforcement or self defense.

But then again, Sarah Connor was serving pancakes and coffee before she started sparring with terminators.

From the corner of my eye, I saw Anthony swing up the steps.

"Mind if I join you?" he asked.

"Yes."

"It was a rhetorical question." He sat on the bar stool next to mine. "Grace, mind if I get a beer?" he asked. He focused on me. "Thinking of your dad?"

"Yes," I lied.

"He cares about you."

"That's fine. But usually fathers of twenty-nine-year-old daughters care by sending birthday cards and inviting them home for Christmas."

Anthony folded over the corner of his napkin.

"All right, then," I said. "What's your story? You're here all alone. I don't see you toting your Mom around."

"You don't want to know."

"You must realize saying that is going to make me desperate to know."

"Of course," he said. "You're a woman."

"What's that supposed to mean?"

"You're so easy."

"Excuse me?"

"Easy to rile up. I see why your dad has so much fun."

"Okay, smart guy. Don't tell me." I looked down at my lemonade and rattled the cubes against the curves in the glass.

"Well, if you really must know."

I tried not to seem too interested.

"I'm here on my honeymoon."

19

I fully expected a woman to stride up and clock me in the jaw.

"Now wait a minute," Anthony said. "Don't get your panties in a bunch. Let me explain."

"I think you better," I said.

"My wedding day was eight months ago."

"That's a pretty long honeymoon," I muttered. "What did you do with your wife? Dump her in a lake?"

"Don't have a wife."

"Now you're making a lot of sense."

"I didn't get married."

"You're going to have to explain that one."

"Let me give you the *Spark Notes* version," he said. "I've always been a traditional kind of guy. Played by the rules. Went to college. Got my Ph.D. Became a professor. Next logical step seemed to be the marriage thing. Kids, whatever."

"You're awfully sentimental."

"Yeah, well. Day of my wedding I thought, I'm going to flaunt tradition and sneak in to see my wife-to-be in her dress before the wedding."

"Bad luck."

"I'd say. Found her in her white dress all right, but it was hiked all the way up around her waist."

"No."

"Fraid so."

"The best man?"

"Not quite that cliché. Ex-boyfriend. Dumped her before I met her, yada, yada."

"Sorry."

"Yeah. Anyway, we were supposed to go to Costa Rica for our honeymoon. My idea. I'd been on a couple of digs in Central America, but never been here. So I came anyway. Spent the entire ten days in a drunken stupor. Thought a lot about what happened and started figuring that maybe the can't-see-the-bride-in-her-dress stuff is an elaborate cover so women can sneak in a fling before the big moment."

I gasped. "That is not true."

"You married?"

"No."

"Ever been?"

"Not even close."

"Well, then. What do you know? Anyway, doesn't matter. The point is I got tired of following tradition, playing by the rules. I called up the dean at my university and requested a leave of absence. Been in Costa Rica ever since."

"I think that's awesome."

"Thanks a lot."

"Not the wedding part. I mean, having the courage to say the heck with everything and make your way in a new country. Try out a new life."

"Maybe." Anthony looked at me thoughtfully for a moment. "You been to the Nicoya Peninsula?"

"No."

"It's north of here, also on the Pacific side. The people there, they have a saying, *plan de vida*. It's a philosophy for how to live."

"Life plan. I had one of those once. Still do, I guess. But other people, well — let's say they have a way of interfering."

"That's not it. You're being too literal."

"What do you mean?"

"It doesn't mean plan *for* life. It means plan *of* life."

"There's a difference?"

"*Plan de vida* is a way of life. It's simple really. You eat sensibly, appreciate small moments, embrace family. In fact, most Costa Ricans wouldn't find it strange that you and your dad are close."

"But we're not—"

"*Plan de vida* also means enjoying what life plans for you. Those unexpected encounters that impart a kind of visceral pleasure to life."

I narrowed my eyes at Anthony. "I think your seize-the-day philosophy could be construed as a little self-serving."

"Oh, trust me. I can be quite good at serving another."

My life plan didn't include an answer to that.

Anthony folded over another corner of his napkin. "They say the Nicoya Peninsula is inhabited by a record number of centenarians," he said.

"Centenarians?"

"People who live to be a hundred or more. I think they might be on to something over there."

"So you want to help me live longer, is that it?"

"No." Anthony spun his bar stool and moved in closer to me. "To help you enjoy your life now."

I tried to trap a cube of ice with my straw.

Anthony watched me.

I willed myself to look him in the eye. "What did you have in mind?"

He leaned towards me in a single, slow, fluid motion, pressed through the boundary that defined my personal space, and grabbed my eyes with his.

"Lose the plan," he said.

And he was gone.

20

Why is every man I meet so cryptic?

Forget Stonehenge and pyramids and mysterious giant spheres. There is nothing as unfathomable as members of the opposite sex. Exactly what plan did Anthony want me to lose? And why did my dad always have to hide his feelings behind goofy jokes? What was Tarzan doing making strange phone calls in the middle of the night? And what did Hector mean when he said that Luis was working on it? What was there to work on? His daughter was missing. Call the police.

Anthony was wrong. What I needed to do now was find a plan. Not lose it. I couldn't just sit around and do nothing. I had traveled this road before. I couldn't let Rosa down the way I had Kaylee. I needed to find out what Luis was doing to bring home his daughter. I needed to figure out what Tarzan was up to and if he was somehow involved.

Maybe I didn't need a plan of life. But I definitely needed a plan of action.

The trouble was, I didn't have any idea where to get one. What did sleuths do at a time like this? A brilliant plan always fell into their heads like a divine blast from the sky. But that wasn't exactly true. Sleuths did stuff, too. They searched for clues. They followed leads. They asked people questions.

As I nursed my lemonade and pondered my plan of action, the cooks laid out lunch. I got up, put a few things on my plate, and went outside to sit on the steps. I didn't want anyone to bother me.

The only clue to Rosa's disappearance was the letter. But I didn't have the letter. In fact, I hadn't even read it. A lot of good that did me.

So how about a lead? I had overheard Tarzan having that weird conversation on the phone right after Rosa was taken. Did that count as a lead? Even if it did, I hadn't seen Tarzan all day. If he traipsed in right now, what would I do? Tail him? Set up a stakeout?

My dad and Anthony were right. I didn't know what I was doing. I was just a writer, after all. I wasn't smart and brave and daring like—

Stop it. That kind of thinking wasn't going to get me anywhere. But what was left? Asking people questions?

That sounded like something I might be able to do. But who? I wouldn't feel comfortable marching up to Luis's front door and interrogating the man. I wasn't a police officer or anything.

That pretty much left Hector. He had to know what was going on. But I would have to get him alone. I didn't want to question him in front of everyone.

Our entire afternoon was going to be taken up with

tours. I needed a chance to talk to Hector alone. I would have to find a way to corner him during a break.

There. I did it. I made a plan.

Sort of.

The rest of the day was spent doing things that ordinarily I would have loved. We started out by touring a small factory. There, women in the village concocted natural shampoos out of native plants. Most of the women did not speak English, yet they welcomed us with warmth and shared the passion they felt for their work. I left cradling a sample of a rich shampoo the women had specially formulated for dark hair. I wondered if the thick goo was the secret to Grace's luxurious tresses.

Throughout the rest of the afternoon, I dutifully listened, jotted down notes, and snapped pictures. As much as everything interested me, my heart just wasn't in it. I was too preoccupied with figuring out how I was going to get Hector alone. An opportunity never presented itself.

By the time we got back to the lodge, evening was settling in. Hector gathered our group together and gave us some instructions for the next day's activity — white-water rafting. Then he turned to leave.

This was it. My chance.

But now that it came to it, I wavered.

Hector strode away from the lodge and disappeared out into the gathering night.

Damn. I was blowing it.

If I didn't do something soon, I was going to miss my chance.

I mentally booted myself in the rear. Then I bounded down the steps and chased Hector down.

He spun on me. "Is there a problem?"

"Uh — no," I said. "No. I was just wondering if maybe I could, uh—"

"Yes?"

"Well, I was just wondering if maybe I could ask you a couple of questions."

"Is this for your article?"

"No."

Hector looked at me expectantly.

"Well, it's just this. I was hoping maybe you could—"

Hector fidgeted. I was beginning to try his patience.

"Can you tell me what's happening with Rosa?"

Hector said nothing.

"Um — please?"

"That is a private matter," he said.

"I know, but—"

"It is not your concern."

"Of course. I'm sorry. You're right. It's just that, well, I haven't seen any police or anything."

"We take care of our own."

"You mean to tell me, Luis didn't call the police?"

"As I said, the matter is private."

"But Rosa is just a little girl. Shouldn't Luis do everything he can to find her?"

Hector bristled. "She will be returned," he said, "as soon as he has the money."

"Luis is going to pay the ransom?" I was shocked.

Hector looked like he'd said something he shouldn't have. "The matter is private."

This time, he meant it. He would say no more.

So much for that plan.

I already needed a new one.

I hadn't executed the first one very well, but at least I had gleaned an important piece of information. Two pieces, actually.

One was that Luis had not involved the police. Two was that he was planning to pay the ransom.

But where was Luis getting the money? The man lived in a shack for crying out loud. The kidnapper must have had a reason to think Luis could get the money. That meant it had to be someone Luis knew. Didn't it?

That line of thinking brought me back to Tarzan. He was a shaky lead, I had to admit, but it was the only one I had. So there it was — my elaborate new plan. Keep an eye on Tarzan.

To do that, I had only one choice.

I was going to have to go rafting.

21

O' dark thirty.

I hated getting up that early. But to be on the river by nine, we had to leave the lodge by six.

We huddled by the front of the lodge, gulping down hastily brewed coffee. Our group this morning consisted of the usual eight plus one extra. Anthony had decided to join us. I liked to think it was because of me.

Our guides for the day were Hector and Tarzan. They pulled up in front of the lodge in a rumbling pick-up truck that might have once been navy blue. Now it was a patchwork of faded paint, gray bondo, and orange rust.

The truck's bed was fenced in by a steel frame. Two inflated yellow rafts perched on top. From the side, they looked like two huge bananas. Bench seats lined either side of the truck's bed.

"Hop in," Tarzan said.

The seating was tight. I wanted to avoid my dad, so I sat sandwiched against the truck's rickety tailgate. The only thing holding the tailgate shut was a piece of bailing wire. But since Anthony completed the sandwich, I didn't really mind the squeeze.

The truck leaped into gear and roared away from the lodge and past the village. Tarzan was behind the wheel. He must have figured the extra speed would propel us over the ruts in the road. It didn't. For two hours, my rear end absorbed every one of them.

We came to an intersection with the highway and I relaxed. At least until it occurred to me that I was speeding over pavement with only a thin piece of wire holding the tailgate — and me — in place.

"Well now," Anthony said.

I barely heard him over the sound of the air whistling through the rafts above our heads. I looked down and realized that my hand was clutching his thigh. I smiled sheepishly. "I'm afraid I might fall out."

Anthony responded by wrapping an arm behind me. He pulled me close and held me tight against his side.

A rush of tingly warmth spread under my skin. I could've stayed like that all day, but a few minutes later, we careened off the paved road. The truck bounded to a stop between a roadside stand and a bridge.

Tarzan and Hector released the tailgate. The nine of us

unpretzeled ourselves, climbed out of the bed, and stretched our cramped limbs.

"Get breakfast here," Tarzan said.

The roadside stand served coffee, surprisingly hot, strong, and good. It also served cold pastries.

With a coffee in one hand and a pastry in the other, I strolled to the bridge and peered over the edge. I saw a muddied expanse of sluggish water. Near the green-fringed bank, something moved.

"What do you see?" Anthony sidled up next to me and leaned over the railing, sipping his coffee.

"I don't like what I think I see."

Anthony whistled. "Is that the river we're going to raft?"

"I'm betting on it."

"Yikes."

Stacy and her entourage of college boys crowded around us. "Whoa," the video-camera-kid said. "Will you get a load of that?" He angled his lens towards the muddy water. "With the zoom on this thing, I can make out their teeth."

"This isn't right," Stacy said. "I thought crocodiles only lived in A places."

"A places?" I asked.

"Yeah, you know," Stacy said. "Australia, Africa, the Amazon."

"I don't think you have anything to worry about," Anthony said. "Crocs don't like white water."

"You know that for sure?" I asked.

"Well," Anthony said, "I guess if they got really hungry..."

I handed him my untouched pastry and hurried back to the truck.

We climbed back into the truck's bed. A distant growl caught our attention. As the sound came closer, it grew into a roar and then into an all-out thunder. A military-style vehicle, with tires that looked like they could traverse the moon, charged towards us.

Just as I thought it would slam into us, the monster truck swerved and zigzagged around us. The canvas-clad bed held twenty or so passengers. They hung over the side and hooted at us. A trailer with three rafts hobbled behind.

"Bastard," Tarzan said.

We settled into our little truck and meekly followed the other.

Shortly after the bridge, we left the smooth asphalt and bumped down another dirt road. Below us on our right, a snaking river flashed its colors at us. At a cut in the bank, the truck nosed down towards the river's slithering belly.

The monster truck was there. Its passengers swarmed the put-in. We parked at a distance and Tarzan sprang the tailgate. We scrambled out of the bed, eager to begin the day's adventure.

Video-camera-kid was already busy. I had left my SLR at the lodge. I couldn't chance having the camera sink to a watery grave at the bottom of the river.

I pulled a plastic zip bag out of my pocket and wandered down to a secluded spot on the bank. Here, the river serpent's belly ballooned outward, as though it had swallowed a huge meal.

I slid my point-and-shoot camera out of the baggie and framed a couple of images. I took a moment to review them.

I wasn't satisfied with the results.

A camera has yet to be invented that can capture what a

place feels like. A camera sees darkness and light, contrast and shade, saturation and hue, but it filters out everything else.

They say that you can't photograph a vampire because it has no soul. But I doubt it would matter if it did. A camera can capture shadows and illuminations, shapes and forms, but it can never quite capture the elusive spirit of a place. No matter the quality of the lens, a camera can't focus on an apparition.

I had started my career as a photographer, but was always frustrated by what the camera left out. Eventually, I discovered that only words could come close to caging the idea of a place. That is why I became a writer.

I reviewed the shots again and decided the missing element was sound. I switched the camera to video-mode so that later I could try to recreate the river's sound with words.

Anytime I wrote about water — its sound, feel, movement, activity, or appearance — I found myself scrounging for the right words. Kaylee once told me that the Inuit — a people who lived in the extreme north — had hundreds of words to describe snow. I often thought water in its liquid form needed a similarly rich vocabulary.

Where was the word for the sound a river made from a distance, like the whoosh of air through the trees? Or when close by it sounded like the drum of rain on a roof? Or closer still, the way its churning sounded like milk shaken in a plastic jug?

As I perched there on the bank, listening to the water's rhythm, it seemed to me that on this day the river pulsed to the sound of two syllables.

Ros—a.

22

Tarzan summoned us.

"Look lively folks," he said. "There're two of us and nine of you. Let's get these rafts off the truck."

I went up on my tippy-toes. I couldn't reach the rafts, so I made a show of being helpful.

Once the rafts were on the ground, Tarzan demanded our full attention. "Here's what's in store for today," he said.

Stacy interrupted him. "Look." She pointed towards the river. "That group's leaving already."

None of us could resist the distraction. We turned and watched as the horde of people from the monster truck swarmed onto three oar boats and blasted down the river.

"Damn foreign outfitter," Tarzan hissed behind us. "Sometimes, those fools run up to six trips a day on this river. All they care about is getting them in, getting them out. They don't let their guests paddle or stop for lunch. Their guides punch through this stretch in an hour. We, on the other hand, take half a day."

Tarzan's outburst refocused our attention. I sensed that he very much wanted to call the other outfitter a bastard again.

Instead, he said, "It's lucky you're with us. This trip's gonna be epic."

Stacy whispered to me. "Epic? The guy sounds pretty foreign himself."

"I heard that." Tarzan fixed his gaze on Stacy's breasts.

Stacy folded her arms over her chest.

"I'm here," Tarzan said, "because when the lodge started runnin' river trips, they needed to bring in a boatman with skills. Me — I've bagged class five rivers all over the world. You see our buddy Hector, here? He's training with the best."

Hector plopped a pile of yellow helmets on the ground.

Stacy whispered again, softer this time "If he's all that, what's he doing with this little outfit? I bet he got himself fired from somewhere else for being an ass."

Or a kidnapper.

"Listen," Tarzan said. "The rafts we'll be using today are fourteen-footers, made of polyurethane, very smooth on the water. Can you see the way the front and back of the raft curves up? That's called the raft's kick. The front of the raft is called the bow. The back, where I sit, is the stern."

Tarzan hopped into the back of the raft and posed. "I like to call this the catapult seat. When we hit a wave, the stern'll snap up like a buckin' bronc. It takes real skill to not get thrown out."

I enjoyed a mental image of Tarzan catapulting through the air.

"Does anyone know what the two inflated tubes in the middle of the raft are called?" he asked.

Silence.

"I thought not. You probably think they look like seats. They're not. Don't sit on them. Those are there to give the raft its shape, not to cushion your butts. They're called thwarts."

Tarzan parked himself on the raft's O-shaped outer tube.

"You have to sit here, on the edge. That way you can paddle and keep the boat balanced. The inside of the outer tube has four chambers. That's so if the raft gets punctured, the whole thing doesn't deflate beneath us like in a Tom and Jerry cartoon."

Tarzan hopped out of the raft.

"Aurora, Stacy, David, Anthony, you're in my boat," Tarzan said, pointing at the closest raft. "The rest of you are in Hector's."

We shuffled towards our rafts.

"Now," Tarzan continued, "I suppose you want to know what you're in for today. The river's pumping at a thousand cfs. That's short for cubic feet per second. The water's up a half foot because of all the rain we've been havin'. That makes it more fun."

I eyed the pumping river with skepticism. More water meant faster water. In my book, that did not equate to more fun.

"The river pinches down in a couple spots," Tarzan said. "With the higher water, a few of the rapids will be a solid class three or four."

"Class what?" Stacy asked.

"Novices," Tarzan muttered. "Let me make this simple for you. White water is classified on a scale of one to six. Ones and twos give you a nice float trip. Threes give you a lot of fun waves to play on. Class fours are where it starts to get serious. Class fives are expert-level. And sixes are off the charts."

"Gosh," Stacy said. "Class four won't be too hard for us novices?" She leaned closer to me and whispered, "How come these guides gotta have their own language?"

"Good question," I said.

When river runners were faced with the dearth of words that described water, they must have decided to invent their own. They had words for the way water moved, words for the way water looked, words for the way water behaved. My personal favorites were the oh-so-comforting words for the different kinds of rapids. Stoppers, keepers, curlers, breakers, haystacks, undercuts, hydraulics, humps, rooster tails, holes, boils.

As far as I was concerned, they might as well have just named them all drowners.

Rivers had a strange push-pull effect on me. They scared the crap out of me, yet I had always been strangely drawn to them. Unlike the oceans, which were stuck in a repetitive motion, rivers seemed to go somewhere. They had a purpose. A mission.

I never liked sitting by the ocean. The tired rolling of the waves always made me restless. I wanted to get on a river and move.

It was the falling in part that scared me.

"Now then," Tarzan was saying. "Safety gear. Hector's set out the helmets and life jackets. Find one that fits. And be quick about it."

We rummaged through the piles. The helmets blazed a bright yellow, the vests a bright orange. "Great," I said to Stacy. "We're going to look like two big tubs of candy-corn floating down the river."

"Raise your hands in the air," Tarzan said. "Have someone cinch down your vest. If you fall out, the vest'll save you." He waggled a finger at Stacy. "Come here."

"Aurora can tighten mine," she protested.

"Just come here."

Stacy edged towards him. "What're you going to do?"

"Kneel on the ground," Tarzan said.

"Excuse me?"

Tarzan swung into one of the rafts. "I'm gonna show you how to pull someone in." He leaned over the outer tube, grabbed Stacy by the front of her vest, and launched his body backwards. He landed inside the raft with Stacy sprawled across his chest.

Stacy scrambled up and in her haste to get away, pitched over the side of the raft.

Tarzan clambered out of the raft after her. "You'll all get to practice that in a few minutes," he said. "First, let's discuss the rapids."

I broke into a sweat inside my helmet and vest.

"The first two rapids," Tarzan said, "are Tranquilo and Cotton Candy. After those, we'll stop for lunch. Then comes the tough ones, Hueco Gringo — which means Gringo's Hole — and El Horrendito."

"El Horrendito?" I repeated.

"Little Horror," Anthony said.

Perfect.

"The rapids on this river can toss you about," Tarzan said, "but they're usually forgiving."

Usually?

Hector approached. He carried two fistfuls of paddles.

"The most important thing," Tarzan said, "is to listen to me. I give the commands."

We selected our paddles.

"This here is no free ride," Tarzan said. "You gotta paddle. Watch me now. I'm gonna show you how to do it. First, put one hand on the T-grip at the end of the handle like this. Put your other hand on the shaft by the blade. Then dig in like this."

Tarzan scooped the air with the paddle.

We did the same.

"The commands I'll be using today are simple. Forward, back, right, left, and stop. Think you can handle that?"

We paddled some more to prove our competence.

"My paddle's longer than yours," Tarzan said. "That's so I can steer. It's also so I can reach forward and whap you if you're not doing it right."

If he was hoping for a laugh, he didn't get one.

"When I say *Right*, those of you on the right side paddle backwards. When I say *Left*, the folks on the left side paddle backwards. Got it? Now let's get in."

We picked up the rafts and carried them down to the water.

"Anthony and David," Tarzan said. "You sit in the middle. Stacy and Aurora, up front."

I stepped into the belly of the raft. Immediately, I lost all sense of the comforting stability of land. The raft was all taut curves and movement. I could feel the river bucking beneath. I took another step. The raft's surface was hard and rubbery and smooth, quite unlike the squishy give of an air mattress. The tension made me feel if I stepped too forcefully or sat too quickly, I would spring straight up and out of the raft.

I settled into the position at the front right and clutched the paddle across my lap. Rafts don't have any handles or loops or grips as being attached to a raft in any manner can have dire consequences. The only way for me to hold on was to ram my toes between the fat oval tube and the floor. Even with my toes tucked snugly under the tube, I felt anything but secure.

The last time I went rafting, I tumbled into the river

and spent a full second trapped beneath the raft, certain I would never escape the weight of the enormous beast bearing down on me. Now the weight of all that happened in the past few days bore down on me.

I had resisted my dad's interference with my life, struggled with my inadequacies, been drawn into a strange sort of dance with Anthony, dreamed a nightmare that was not my own, and projected every fear and suspicion about Rosa's kidnapping onto Tarzan. Even the friendly squabbling between the college kids as they boarded their raft seemed full of conflict.

The tension of it all left me feeling as taut and unyielding as the raft.

23

"Get out."

We had finally climbed into the raft and practiced a few paddle strokes in the eddy.

Now Tarzan was telling us to get out.

We turned and looked at him.

"What're you gawkin' at?" he said. "I told you we were gonna practice rescues. Now get out."

We turned and looked at each other.

"You sorry bunch of wusses. You're just gonna get wet anyway."

In a flash, Tarzan upended Anthony. He tumbled ass-over-head into the water.

Anthony surfaced next to the raft. "Why you—" He caught himself when he saw everyone staring. He tipped onto his back and floated. "Come on," he said. "The water's great. It's hot as blazes in those vests."

We slithered into the water before Tarzan could dump us overboard. Anthony was right. The cool water was a relief.

Tarzan leaned over the side of the raft. "Ladies first." He reached for Stacy.

She moved away. "You go." She pushed me closer to the raft.

"Thanks a lot."

Tarzan pulled me in and chucked me off to the side. He left me lying in the bottom of the raft and beckoned to Stacy.

I got up in time to see her swim to the raft. Tarzan reached out and grabbed her by the chest. He pulled her straight back, forcing her to sprawl over the top of him again.

"That's how it's done," Tarzan said. "Even weak women like you can pull a big, strong man like me into the boat. Go ahead, give it a try."

Stacy and I positioned ourselves on either side of the raft.

"That guy's such a jerk," Stacy said. She leaned over the outer tube. "I'll take care of your dad. You get Mr. Ripped."

Anthony kicked himself over to the raft. "Help me," he said. "I'm drowning."

I didn't want to make a fool of myself, so I tugged at his vest with all my might.

Anthony launched into the air and landed on top of me. He pressed me into the bottom of the raft with the entire length of his body. "That was sexy," he said against my ear. "You saved my life."

"Get off me." I tried to shove him away.

Anthony winked and took his time getting up.

We resumed our positions on the raft. Water sheeted off our bodies and pooled under our rear ends.

"Listen up," Tarzan said. "If you can't manage to stay in the raft today—" I was sure he was talking to me. "Then here are some emergency procedures to remember."

I paid close attention. Emergency procedures were always important for me.

"If you take a swim, lift your legs and point them downstream. That way your feet don't get trapped down below. I'll toss you this throw bag." Tarzan held up a red polyester bag. "A rope's coiled inside. It'll spool out as it flies through the air. Don't be stupid and grab the bag, though. You have to hold the rope."

Yeah, Aurora. Don't be stupid.

"Let's hit it," Tarzan said. "First thing we've gotta do is pierce the eddy line. That's where the main current slides past the eddy. Then we'll be in the middle of it. Hang on."

Tarzan barked his commands.

A few forward strokes brought us into the main current. We shot down the river, straight towards the white water.

At its worst, navigating white water is like trying to drive to work after an earthquake has heaved the road into rubble. Your car is pushed along by an unstoppable force. You have no brakes or power steering, only a paddle with which to maneuver. Bridges have broken away, leaving vertical drops as high as a house. The road is hemmed on either side by skyscrapers that narrow the world into a slim canyon.

There's no place to pull off for a rest. There's only jagged debris and rock-hard obstacles and bone-smashing rubble. And over all this pours a frothy, churning rage of liquid.

Luckily for us, the river was not at its worst.

That would come later.

For now, the river advanced in a stately manner, permitting the raft to skim along its surface. The river meandered to the left and the boat snuggled up against the left bank. Then, since nature has an eye for symmetry, the river meandered to the right and we glided to the opposite side.

The raft's movement felt the way I imagined a magic carpet ride through the clouds would be. Soaring and dipping. Dipping and soaring.

"Tranquilo," Tarzan said.

We floated over riffles of white water and sailed across a section of green-blue water that stretched the river wide.

"Now we're approachin' Cotton Candy." Tarzan said. "It gets its name from the sugary threads of water that spin at the base of the drop."

I raised an eyebrow in surprise. Who would have thought the pompous-ass of a guide could be so eloquent? I knew then that rivers were his love.

Tarzan angled the raft into the head of the rapid. The river narrowed. We bump-bump-bumped down a slippery slide. In front of us, the water and the horizon joined into one. The river seemed to end, plunging into nothingness. Then we were upon it, the spun sugar sifting below us.

We tipped over the rim. For a moment, we hovered in the liquid air above the liquid water and I was filled with the power of the river's purpose as it moved towards an unseen destination, smoothing over rough spots and scouring the world clean, pushing through tiny cracks and carving mighty canyons and filling them with the magic of water going through its cycles and fueling the weather and feeding life.

And I was part of it all, going along for the ride and becoming part of the river's purposeful existence.

The bow of the boat nosed down into the frothy softness that floated above the surface. A cool spray misted across my face. It tasted of pulverized rock and soaked-up sunshine.

Around me, whoops of joy erupted from the other passengers. The stern slapped down. We moved as one entity over a great swell and a wave kicked us to one side and then the river — having no time to pause and reflect — carried us towards our next challenge. I accepted its call with a soaring soul and laughed out loud at the sheer pleasure of it all.

The raft drifted free of the rapid and skated into a wide pool. Sunlight gilded the surface. The flat water shined like gold leaf.

You know something, Aurora?
Kaylee — you pick the strangest times.
I wanted to tell you my favorite saying.
Okay, then.
Life isn't measured by the number of breaths you take.
No?
It's measured by the moments that take your breath away.
I miss you, Kaylee.
I'm here.

The guides nudged the rafts onto the beach.
We disembarked.
"Stretch your legs," Tarzan said. "We'll set up for lunch. Be back in fifteen."

The guides unloaded the gear from the rafts. They

perched a fold-out table on the bank and started setting out the lunch items.

I took my camera and wandered downstream. As I worked at composing my shots, the mystery of Rosa's disappearance gnawed.

Tarzan didn't act like someone who'd just kidnapped a girl. But then, what would he act like if he did? I didn't actually have a good reason to suspect him. So what if I had heard him on the phone? He could have been talking about anything.

And yet that first night, at the lodge, Tarzan had been so attentive to Rosa, helping her get dinner and find a chair. Was he trying to win her over so she'd trust him? Or was he just being nice? The whole thing was driving me crazy. Maybe my dad was right. Maybe I should just butt out.

The jungle rustled behind me. "Anthony."

"Am I disturbing you?" he asked.

"Not really."

We sat next to each other at the edge of the water.

"You're pretty when you concentrate like that," he said.

I shifted away. "I'm not."

"You are."

We silently contemplated the river.

"The ride's going to get wilder," Anthony said.

"I'm ready."

He reached up, skimmed a few strands of hair off my neck, and kissed along my hairline. My pulse skipped like a rapid.

"Lunch is on." My dad said from behind our backs.

"Your father has impeccable timing," Anthony murmured.

"Tell me about it."

24

*H*ector held a long-bladed knife in his hand.

The group gathered in a semi-circle. We watched as he plucked a whole pineapple from the picnic table. He held it by the prickly tufts and laid the fruit on its side at the edge of the table. With the knife, he lopped the pineapple down the middle. The two halves rolled apart.

Using the tip of the blade, Hector cut the tender meat inside the pineapple into squares. He jabbed the point into a chunk and held it out to me. I took the juicy cube. Its tart sweetness melted on my tongue.

Then Tarzan handed out reusable plastic plates. We loaded the plates with cold chicken, macaroni salad, slaw, and pineapple. Hector passed out cool cups of lemonade. We rested on the beach, ate our lunch, and watched the busy river go by.

After lunch, the guides gathered everything up, re-rigged the rafts, and coaxed us back into the boats.

"Okay folks," Tarzan said when we'd hitched a ride on the current. "We've got some slow water here. Up ahead's where she gets crazy. Give me two forwards strokes."

We paddled twice.

"That's good."

We rested.

"Wanna hear something interesting?" Tarzan didn't bother to wait for an answer. "I guided a trip in the States and there was this guy. He was a hydro—, hydrol—, hell, I don't remember. A water guy. He told me rivers are made up of three kinds of water. The fun, white stuff is called turbulent and chaotic water. Isn't that a kick? Turbulent and chaotic are real terms in hydro—"

"Hydrology," Anthony said.

"Yeah, that's it. The slow stuff we're in right now is called. Oh hell, what'd he call it? Laminated."

"Laminar," Anthony said.

I couldn't resist peeking back at Anthony. Despite the goofy helmet and life vest, he looked sexier than ever. I wished I could sit behind him and watch his bare arms flex against the current. I smirked inwardly, thinking of Stacy's pet word. Ripped.

"Whatever," Tarzan said. "This guy told me that river water moves in sheets. The top and bottom sheets are slower because of drag from the air and the river bed. The sheet that lies just beneath the surface moves the fastest. You can feel it if you stick your paddle in."

The four of us plunged our blades into the river's dark core. I felt the water tug the paddle forward in my hands.

"That's cool," Stacy said. "It's like something's alive down there."

Rivers, it seemed, were like people. You could never tell by looking at the surface what lay beneath.

"You folks don't know how easy you have it," Tarzan said. "This raft is a modern self bailer. Used to be, somebody'd have to shovel all the water out with a bucket. By the way—that'd be one of you fine ladies up front."

Thank goodness it wasn't up to me to keep the raft afloat.

"Back in the day," Tarzan continued, "people used to run rivers facing backwards instead of forwards."

"Yeesh," I said to Stacy. "Doesn't sound much different from the way I raft. Close my eyes. Hope for the best."

"Maybe there's something to be said for that." Stacy eyed the river ahead. "Then you can't see what's coming. Looks like we're about to hit some of that chaos."

A white squall line loomed on the water's horizon.

"Hueco Gringo," Tarzan said. "Pay attention now. This hole's pretty grabby. The current's gonna draw us left, but there's a car-sized boulder there, so we're gonna cut right to get around the hole. Oh — I forgot to tell you one thing."

That can't be good.

"If we wrap on a rock," Tarzan said, "I'll tell you to *Highside*. That means if the raft starts to flip, jump over to the high side. That's the only way we're gonna make it."

A fine time to tell us this crucial piece of information.

"Now remember everythin' I said earlier," Tarzan said. "I command. You obey. And I don't want to see any flailin' maniacs out there. Whatever you do, don't fall out."

Right.

Don't fall out. Don't fall out. Don't fall out.

We followed Tarzan's commands and slipped effortlessly around the boulder. But as we angled towards the right, something went wrong. The high water pushed us forward too fast. We headed for the hole.

Holes are kind of like tigers.

When they're babies, they're cute and cuddly and non-threatening.

Baby holes are found in creeks where water flows over the tops of rocks and then flips over backwards. It's the downward pull of the backward-flowing wave that creates the hole. In creeks, holes are so tiny a child can surf a rubber-duckie or a toy-boat or a flip-flop on top.

When flowing water reaches class three status, holes become large enough for rafts to surf, creating a fun diversion for paddlers.

But at class four levels, holes become dangerous, trapping rafts and flipping them and sucking swimmers into their murky depths.

At class five, holes can be as lethal as the full-grown tiger. These giant churning vortexes are known as keepers.

Keepers can hold a raft in its clutches for hours or even days. A person unlucky enough to be trapped inside a keeper hole will circulate like a sock in a washing machine. The body may not surface for a week.

Thankfully for us, this river was not a full-grown class five. Class four would prove to be more than enough.

"Right. Right!" The hard edge in Tarzan's voice propelled us into action.

We dug deep.

The raft crawled a few feet to the right, but we didn't make it.

We stalled on top of a lurking black rock and teetered on the edge of the hole. White water roiled below us. The powerful backwash curled inward on itself. The raft tipped forward.

I leaned back, feeling like a ball about to be caught in a mitt.

The raft slid over. We dropped into the depression, wheeled about, and spun sideways. The submerged rock loomed on our left. The backwards curling wave crashed on our right. Water hammered the tube.

The raft joggled like a bug trapped in a hot tub jet.

My dad and I inched away from the pounding water.

"No," Tarzan shouted. "Highside!"

The tube on the front right lifted, slowly at first, then higher and higher. The river gathered its strength as it prepared to flip us.

Anthony and my dad and Tarzan lunged forward, trying to redistribute the weight in the raft. The tube lowered somewhat, but the river was not to be dissuaded. Its grasping fingers reached over the stern and gave it a sharp tug.

The men did not have a good hold on the raft.

They slipped, one-by-one, into the dark hole.

25

The hole swallowed the three men.

The stern popped up, buoyed by its newfound lightness. The bow rode high on the wave that curled back into the hole.

Stacy and I clung to the raft's slippery surface like two ants trying not to slip off a wet leaf.

The raft leveled and spun.

I clung to the jackhammering tube and scanned the water ahead. I couldn't find any sign of the men. Fear clutched in my chest. Where were they? Trapped beneath the raft? Circulating in the depths of the hole?

I reached out with my paddle and stirred the water. Nothing happened.

I came to a sickening realization. Paddling inside the deep depression was not going to get us anywhere. We had to find a way to reach beyond its grasp.

The water punched and pummeled and pounded.

Then, in a snapping twist of fate, the forces of nature turned in our favor. The river knocked the bow forward. We faced downstream.

An escape route momentarily before us, I hollered above the drumming of the river. "Forward!"

Stacy and I lunged across the front of the tube, reached beyond the backwash, and dug into the main current. The raft shivered over the lip.

"Again," I shouted. The stern rose. I turned my head to the side and out of the corner of my eye, I saw something that made my blood run cold.

The other raft.

I spun my head back around. "Forward. Forward!" Stacy and I dug in harder. But the other raft came on too fast. I had a fleeting vision of the fourteen-foot beast flopping down on our heads, crushing us beneath its weight and the weight of its six passengers.

Our stern came up a little more. We rode the backwards flowing wave. I thought we were going to make it out. But the river mercilessly shoved us back. Stacy and I lost all the ground we'd gained. I looked around and met the eyes of the college kids and the newlyweds, their faces twisted in fear.

Hector ruddered his boat towards us, his face calm and determined.

They hit us.

Our raft lurched forward. Straight out of the hole.

Hector's raft ricocheted away and shot out beside us, going backwards.

Stacy and I were free of the buffeting hole, but we were

far from safe. The raft fired down the river, speeding towards the next rapid. Once again, I scanned the river ahead for the three men. I could see little through the sloshing water.

"Where are they?" I shouted to Stacy.

"I don't know!"

The raft see-sawed. It pitched backwards and forwards as we bulldozed through one standing wave and then another and then still another.

The motion I had found so comforting before — the dipping and soaring, soaring and dipping — now caused waves of nausea to wash over me. A hard knot lodged in my throat. I tried to swallow it back.

Spray coming off the bow misted my vision. I peered through, trying to capture a glimpse of the three we'd lost in the hole. It was like trying to peer through a rain-streaked windshield. All I could make out was the heaving water and slanting shoreline and lurching banks.

Where was my father? The thought of his body wringing out in the hole sickened me until I thought I would retch. I could not fathom how much time had passed but it was far too long for someone to be under water. Surely by now, he would have stopped breathing. Surely by now, he would have—

I couldn't complete the thought. I became vaguely aware that beside me Stacy was trying to paddle on her own, that we were rushing down the river too fast, that we needed to turn or stop or—

There.

Was that a daub of yellow in the thrashing gray water? It vanished as the bow rode up and over another wave and then it was there again. A yellow daub. A helmet, bobbing.

And another. Two helmets. Where was the third?

Stacy saw the helmets, too. "We have to reach them," she cried.

I knew it was a terrible way to think, but I couldn't help hoping the two helmets belonged to my father and Anthony. A person who could prioritize life like that must be terrible at her core. But I couldn't help it.

My dad had come on this trip because of me. I had been so worried about him worrying about me, I never even considered the possibility that something might happen to him.

And Anthony, hadn't he come rafting because of me? I didn't know that for sure, but what if he had? I couldn't be responsible for another person's death. Not like with Kaylee. I couldn't survive that again.

The gray water and the blue sky and the green shore ran together like a watercolor spattered by rain. I sagged against the raft and might have allowed myself to drift over the side but then it was there. A third daub of yellow, bobbing in a flat eddy behind a massive boulder.

My hands clutched the paddle as my resolve solidified. I recovered my bearings. It was then that I became aware of the danger.

The next rapid. El Horrendito. Little horror.

The looming rapid filled me with big horror.

Stacy and I needed to make that eddy. But we didn't have a crew. Or a captain. And in a matter of moments, we would be in the midst of another powerful rapid.

We did the only thing we could — dug deep into the water and into our reserves, pushing the raft away from the main flow. My muscles screamed against the weight of the river. As we drew closer to the eddy, I saw we were not going to make it. We needed to turn. We needed to turn fast.

Entering an eddy is extremely tricky. A speeding raft has a lot of inertia to overcome. It's like barreling down a highway and trying to swerve into a rest stop without slowing down. If the water is turbulent enough, the eddy line turns into an eddy fence. It takes the coordinated efforts of an entire paddle crew to punch through a barrier like that.

All we had were the two of us.

"Right!" I back paddled hard. Stacy forward paddled. But the raft merely shuddered to the right. No matter how much we pitted our strength against the current, the two of us were never going to create the momentum we needed to propel ourselves into the eddy.

We shot past the men. The three yellow helmets converged in the shelter of the eddy. I could see their faces now. I could hear them shouting. We were so close.

The raft plowed headlong into a rock. The impact threw Stacy and I forward. We scuttled backward so we wouldn't pitch over the bow.

The collision provided the deceleration we needed.

The impatient river shoved at the stern. If we didn't move fast, the raft would spin off the rock. Then it would sprint down the river backwards.

We struggled to paddle. The boat pivoted ninety degrees. The current dragged at the stern. This was our last chance.

We heaved our bodies forward, straining to move the raft before the river whipped us away from the rock, down the river, and into the waiting rapid.

In an instant, the raft jumped forward. It punched through the eddy fence. We swirled into the reversed current. Stacy and I collapsed towards the center of the raft, exhausted.

The men groped for the sides of the raft, trying to find handholds. The eddy was deep, they had no place to stand.

Stacy and I pulled my dad and Anthony into the raft. They, in turn, pulled Tarzan on board.

The guide took his position at the stern. "Nice paddling," he said, but his tone was not friendly.

Stacy ignored him. "Girls rule." She beamed at me and lifted her hand for a high five.

I felt a jolt of joy and returned the high five. I had stayed in the raft after all.

"This river must be a girl," Anthony said, "cause she's damn bitchy."

26

Bitchy or not, we were at the river's mercy.

As soon as we were moving again, the sloped banks fell away and the world narrowed into a slim canyon. The river galloped through the narrow opening like a horse bolting for freedom.

As riders, we were powerless to tame her. All we could do was match her gait as she charged forth on her relentless search for the wide blue sea.

Now our only way out of here was the stampeding body of water.

The experience in the hole had shaken me, but the fact that I had managed to stay in the raft buoyed my spirits.

Added to that the fact that everyone was safe, and I was positively elated.

We approached the last set of rapids.

"El Horrendito," Tarzan said. "You don't wanna swim this one."

The effort I had expended in the hole took its toll. My right leg cramped. We still had a second before we hit the rapid, so I quickly pulled my foot out of the crevice where I had wedged it. I stretched out my leg, twirling my ankle one way, then the other. I let go of my paddle with one hand and reached down. I kneaded the muscles in my calf and along my outer thigh. I stretched it again. The tightness started to work itself out. I was getting ready to tuck my foot back under the tube when we hit the rock.

The raft bounced off the obstacle and jigged to the left. My paddle slipped from my hand. I flopped backwards over the tube. My legs hit the water. I did not go under.

Instead, I bounded along with the raft, my cheek pressed against the tube's slick side.

As I waded through the sudden shock of the fall, I became aware that someone's hand held me against the raft.

I looked up. My dad was twisted over the side. He held me by a strap on my vest. "Get in," he hollered. He tried to reach his other hand around to me, but the raft plowed through a wave. The instant the raft crested, my dad jerked me up.

The combined momentum sent me rocketing over the raft.

My dad gripped my vest harder. I flipped over in mid-air. I sailed above the raft, my legs flailing over my head.

I thwapped back down into the water on the other side of the raft. My dad sprawled across the floor, his arm flung over the tube between Stacy and Anthony. He held me fast.

I struggled to push away from the heaving raft. "Let go!" Water swarmed in as soon as I opened my mouth and the words came out in a garbled splutter. Arms stretched towards me through the frothy water.

"It's too late," Tarzan shouted above the river's roar. "Let her go."

I parted from the raft and slid into the watery depths below.

Bubbles of trapped sunlight swarmed around me. I tumbled in the water and under the foam and I couldn't see the raft and I couldn't breathe and I couldn't find the air. And then my life jacket remembered its job and popped me to the surface.

The muffled world beneath gave way to the roar above. The river raged. People shouted. I bore down on the next rapid.

Lift your legs and point them downstream. The river tossed my legs and dragged them down and whipped them about. I could not lift them.

The forward momentum of the water shoved me closer to the brink.

The thought of flushing through the rapid face down filled me with terror and adrenaline and a surge of will. I wrenched my hips forward and my legs soared up through the water and I was on my back. My toes poked up through the surface just as I crested a wave.

I was in the rapid.

I crashed through a regiment of standing waves, row after row after row. As the waves engulfed me and released me over and over and over, the world swirled with blue sky and green water and white foam and up ahead, a beacon of orange and yellow.

I blasted through a chute that swerved between two boulders, pounded down a staircase of underwater ledges, and washed over a drop. The river swallowed me again. The blackness made a bubble of panic rise. Then the river spit me into a jade pool and in my mind I swam for the shore, but my arms and legs would not respond and I ricocheted off a rock and bumped down a washboard of small but fast-moving rapids.

My legs flailed behind me again and the river widened and shallowed and my knees and shins and toes struck the rocks below and then the worst happened.

The river pinched through a narrow channel flanked by boulders and in its hurry to get by, the water picked up speed and rushed along and my right leg hung and my foot wedged into something below. In an instant I knew what it meant to be an obstacle in a river.

Once I stopped flowing with its natural course, the water saw me as an opposing force and railed against me, ramming me forward and under and bashing me and berating me. I could not overcome its assault. I submerged face down into the river. The water piled at my back.

I struggled, but I could not find the air and my lungs burned and the river boiled around me and in that moment I knew that I would drown. I could not overcome the weight of the water.

A single gallon of water weighs eight pounds. A cubic foot of water weighs sixty-two pounds. When a river rushes along at one-thousand cubic feet per second, it's like having a column of water one-square-foot wide by a thousand-feet long crushing down on you.

I was trapped by thousands of pounds of pressure. Luckily, most of that force flowed around me.

Otherwise, I would have been crushed outright.

The muscles in my arms, neck, and back strained and weakened. Then, slowly, they gave out altogether. Darkness tinged the edges of my vision. A haze crept over my consciousness. My lungs released. Water flowed in.

Visions of crocodiles danced in my head.

Life was a fragile thing. So easy to lose. So easy to take. So slow to come. So quick to pass. I didn't want to die in this river. I still had so many things to see.

My vest jerked backwards.

My head floated above the water. Air seared into my lungs. Coughs racked my body.

I twisted in the river to find my rescuer.

Anthony. He'd propped himself on a rock to hold us against the relentless onslaught of the river.

The red throw bag arced through the air.

Anthony lunged for it and grabbed it and then he flipped me onto my back and we were moving through the water, his arm wrapped tight around me, his other clutching the rope.

We sliced through the current at an angle until we broke into an eddy where the river relaxed. I found my footing in the shallow pool, struggled to stand, and sputtered as I tried to catch my breath.

The water did little to cool the flames in my cheeks.

"Are you all right?" Anthony asked.

"I'm fine." The eyes of the others burned into me. "Just tell everyone to stop staring. I'm fine." That was technically true, though I could feel bruises forming on my legs and on my ego.

Anthony waved at the others in the raft, letting them

know I was okay. He held out a hand. "Let me help you."

"No."

"Hey," he said. "I saved your life. You're beholden to me."

"A regular knight in shining-orange life vest."

"Suit yourself." He left me sulking in the water.

I had never been so humiliated, even by my dad, and that was saying a lot. Stacy pulled me into the raft. She sensed my embarrassment and did not fuss over me.

During the long drive back to the lodge, I tried not to dwell on what happened. I forced myself to focus on the moments that took my breath away. Slowly, my embarrassment dissipated.

After a shower and dry clothes, I was positively tranquil. I reveled at the night sky as I ambled down the path that wound along the side of Tico's pool.

Happy chatter floated out of the lodge. I was glad everyone was having such a great time. I had a smile on my face when my foot lighted on the bottom step of the lodge.

By the time my foot reached the top step, the smile was gone.

The lights in the lodge were off. A column of speckled light flowed out of a digital projector. The light speared through the darkness, ending in a massive rectangle of brightness on the lodge's one wall.

The white glow of the image lit the happy faces of the onlookers. I tried to sneak back down the stairs, but someone saw me.

"There she is!"

A cluster of people swarmed around me and bore me forward. A beer appeared in my hand and all around me more beers raised above my head in a toast.

I stared in utter mortification at the image on the wall. There, white as snow, larger than life, flailing across the wall, above the rest of my body, over the yellow river raft, were my legs.

The paused image began to move.

My legs flapped in the air as they arced over the boat and plunged down into the heaving water. Then my legs shot back out of the river and jettisoned over the raft in fast reverse.

The jubilant crowd watched the video twenty-seven times.

I know. I counted.

27

Clinomania.

Yes. That was the one.

I loved words. I loved the way some words sounded like what they meant: zip, ping, zoom, splat. I loved the way words arranged in the right sequence — like notes in a musical score — could paint a picture, evoke a mood, or conjure an emotion.

Words were definitions for moments. And the word for that moment was clinomania.

It meant an excessive desire to stay in bed.

As soon as I woke, the image of white legs flailing across the wall flashed over and over against the back of my eyelids. If it hadn't been so hot, I would have burrowed under the covers and stayed there for weeks.

As it turned out, Stacy wouldn't have allowed it. The door to the room burst open. A blast of sunshine and hot air rushed over me.

Stacy slammed the door and plunked herself at the foot of my bed. "Get up sleepy head," she said. "I've already showered and dressed and been to breakfast."

"I don't want to get up." I pulled a pillow over my head.

"Come on now." Stacy tore the sheet off of me. "No sulking. Up and at 'em."

"How many cups of coffee have you had?"

"None. Now come on." She grabbed the pillow off my head and tossed it aside.

"I hate you."

"No you don't. Now get up. I have just the cure for you. Let's go shopping."

"Shopping?"

"A little retail therapy is just what the doctor ordered."

Stacy managed to coax me out of bed. While I took a shower, she went back to the lodge to get me some fruit and coffee. I started to feel a little better.

"Where are we going?" I asked.

"I was checking out the playground like you said. I found this cute little shop. The lady that runs it doesn't speak much English, but she's sweet. She gave me this bracelet even though I didn't buy anything." Stacy held up her arm. A wristlet made of smooth chocolate-colored seed pods slid over her arm.

"It's pretty."

"Isn't it great? I told her I'd be back and that I'd bring a friend."

"Oh, fine. Make me feel guilty."

We set off from the bungalow. Tico slapped the water in greeting — or maybe it was a warning — as we strolled by. I saw Grace in the lodge cleaning up after the breakfast rush. I spun away and picked up my pace. I didn't want anyone to see me yet. Shopping would be the best form of avoidance.

This was true even though I wasn't exactly what you would call a shopaholic. A sleepaholic maybe, but not a shopaholic.

I wouldn't have known a Louis Vuitton from a — oh jeez, I didn't even know what to compare a Louis Vuitton to. I found cavernous box stores frightening on the level of shark infested waters. Don't even get me started on malls. The endless maze of stores and supremely coifed retail staff always had me running for the nearest exit.

Stacy would have a convulsive fit if she knew I did most of my clothes shopping at the local Goodwill. Then again, I bet she could tell. Thankfully, she had enough class not to say so.

That being said, it didn't mean I hated shopping. I would browse the booths of the local farmer's market for hours just to look at the fat tomatoes, drippy peaches, crisp baguettes, puffy kettle corn, hand-knitted baby booties, and dishcloths crocheted by blue-haired grannies.

And when I traveled, I was all about labels. Though I wouldn't have recognized a Louis Vuitton if I woke up in bed with him, I could ferret out a *Made in China* souvenir quicker than a man could think of sex.

I knew all the tricks. Cute little country birdhouse fashioned out of wood and hand-painted with teddy bears and lacy hearts? Flip that sucker over and nine times out of ten there's a *Made in China* stamp cleverly disguised by a knot or whorl in the wood. Maybe granny painted it herself, but to me, if the wood didn't grow practically in her back yard, it was like buying knock-offs on a street corner.

Souvenir shops were as canny as the fake-Rolex and pirated-DVD hawkers that disappeared like smoke when the cops came around. Authentic-looking merchandise would proudly announce 'Designed in Costa Rica' and boast a lovely photo of the native artist, but if you looked close, printed in microscopic print under the 'Designed in—' part, it said *Made in China.*

Maybe I didn't give a jot about designer labels, but that did not mean I wasn't label conscious. I never wanted to be caught dead with a knock-off either. I wanted the real thing.

Stacy and I reached the shop. It consisted of a long table filled with crafts — genuine handmade items — and a woman sitting in a chair with her hands folded over an ample figure.

"Bienvenidos," the woman said.

Stacy and I returned the greeting and moved down the length of the table. We oohed and aahed over little wood jewelry boxes, seed pod necklaces, and feathers painted with pictures of macaws and flowers and waterfalls.

"You with Luis?" the woman asked after a while.

"Yes. Well, we were," I said. "Now his nephew is guiding us."

"Sí, Hector. Good boy. He love village. He work for Luis since his mom and dad sell land and move to city." The woman eyed Stacy. "He is cute, no?"

Stacy blushed. "Sí."

We bought a dozen souvenirs between us, including several bottles of the thick, botanic shampoo. I felt a twinge of guilt as I handed the woman a small stack of colones. Not for spending too much. For spending too little. The prices seemed too low for the amount of time that must have gone into creating each piece. I told her to keep the change.

Stacy and I made our way back towards the lodge. For the time being, I had succeeded in shoving my troubles to the back of my mind. But I knew they wouldn't stay there for long.

"So have you?" Stacy asked.

I must have been lost in thought. I had no idea what she was talking about. "Have I what?"

"Shagged Mr. Tall, Dark, and Chocolate?"

"Shagged? What are you British now?"

"Can you think of a better word?" Stacy swung her bag of souvenirs at her side. "I mean 'do him' sounds like you're going to give him a perm and blond highlights."

"You're crazy, you know that?"

"If you say 'sleep with,' that's a total lie. You're doing just the opposite of sleeping."

"Really crazy."

"'Make love' doesn't work. You haven't known him long enough for that. 'Screw' is something you do when you build a dog house or a fence. 'Getting it on' — well, that sounds like you're going to break into a groovy dance. 'Lie with' sounds like you're an old fuddy duddy in a hoop skirt. And it's definitely too crude to say f—"

"I think you've read one too many sex scenes in those romance novels of yours."

"Come on — shag is perfect. It sounds like you're going to get all hot and sweaty on the shag carpet."

"I'll let you know if I find any shag carpeting around here."

"You're no fun. If you don't go for Mr. Ripped pretty soon, I might go after him."

"He's too old for you."

"So you say."

"Besides," I said. "Won't that shoot *Ripped Night* all to hell?"

"I can change the names to protect the innocent."

"Something tells me you're anything but innocent."

"You got me there," Stacy said. "In fact, I was thinking. That guy, Hector, he is cute, no?"

28

I had more important things to worry about than my legs in the air.

It was time I held my head high and showed my face again. I left Stacy and my shopping bags in the room. I picked up my point-and-shoot camera and headed for the lodge.

Lunch wasn't ready yet, so I settled into a chair and pulled out my camera. I wanted to sort through the pictures I had taken on yesterday's raft trip. The plastic baggie had been tucked into my life vest, and miraculously, the camera survived my unexpected swim.

As I reviewed the photos, Hector came in. He went to the bar and spoke with Grace. He said something about Luis, but I couldn't make it out.

A moment later, Grace said, "I will have them wait for

you here."

I assumed 'them' meant us, the tour group. An impulse made me spring out of my chair and follow Hector. He walked towards the village at a brisk pace. I followed way behind, just barely keeping him in sight.

In a flash of absurdity, I realized I was tailing him. An idea I had thought ridiculous only a couple of days before when I had considered following Tarzan. I didn't know what I would do when Hector got where he was going, but I figured I would worry about that later.

Hector reached the village and headed for the playground. It was a school day. The equipment was empty.

Luis stepped out from behind a twisty slide. He and Hector began to speak in earnest. I ducked behind some trees and tried to listen. I was too far away. I couldn't make out what they were saying.

The shop Stacy and I had visited that morning was adjacent to the playground. I walked to the shop in a wide arc that kept me out of view. I sidled up the front steps and slipped over to the end of the porch. Vines crawled up the side and over the roof, making a kind of screen. From this position, I could hear Luis and Hector. There was just one problem.

They spoke in Spanish.

My hopes plummeted. I knew a few Spanish words and phrases from growing up in New Mexico, but the two men were speaking way too fast for me to discern anything. I thought they said the word *dinero*, money, but I couldn't be sure.

I remembered the camera in my pocket.

Quickly, I pulled it out and poked the little lens through the vines. I zoomed in on Hector and Luis and then I changed the camera to video mode. I hoped the tiny microphone would pick up the sound. I became afraid that the shop keeper would come out and find me spying. I was sure she had noticed me when I slunk by the open door.

Hector and Luis did a lot of pointing and gesturing and headshaking as they talked. They were in disagreement about something.

Behind me, I heard a sound inside of the shop. Like a chair scraping across the floor.

I swiveled my head and listened. I didn't hear anyone approaching.

I turned back to watch Luis and Hector. They started to nod and talk in less excited tones. Some sort of decision had been reached.

Feet creaked across the floor inside the shop.

Hector and Luis were winding down their conversation, but I did not want to miss a critical piece of information. I continued to record their discussion while simultaneously listening behind me. The door had only been partially ajar when I went by.

Now it swished all the way open.

Hector clapped Luis on the shoulder.

Through the soles of my sandals, I felt a vibration in the floor boards. I knew that the shop owner was now standing on the porch behind me. The way I was positioned, my body blocked the view of my camera.

I shut off the recorder and shoved the camera in my pocket just as the woman swung her bulk down the porch towards me. I arranged my face in a neutral expression and rotated around. A chair sat between us. I bent over and ran my hands over the wood, pretending to admire the craftsmanship.

I managed to escape without raising any suspicions. I hurried back to the lodge with my hand cupped protectively over the camera in my pocket. I regarded the video as important evidence. The only problem was, I had no idea how to translate what I had heard.

For the second time in two days, Anthony came to my rescue. He played back the video several times. The sound was surprisingly clear. Anthony paused the video here and there, jotted down notes, and rewound certain parts until he was satisfied that he understood what had been said.

"How do you know Spanish so well?" I asked him, though what I really wanted to know was what he had translated.

"I live in California," he said. "A lot of people are bilingual, especially my students. I took a few classes."

I strained to read his notes. "Wait a minute," He moved his arm over the sheet of paper. "What are you planning to do with this information?"

I was afraid he'd ask that. I tried to look cool and disinterested. "I just want to know what's going on."

"You're a lousy liar," he said. "Not to mention nosy."

"Don't you think you've called me enough names?" I was annoyed that he wouldn't tell me what Luis and Hector were talking about.

"I haven't said anything that's not true," he said.

"Just because you run away from problems, doesn't mean I do."

"That's a crappy thing to say."

"Are you going to tell me, or what?"

"Fine." Anthony uncovered his notes. "They were talking about money."

"Thanks. I figured that much out for myself. What did

they say specifically?"

"They argued over whether or not Luis should go through with it."

"They actually discussed trading the money for Rosa?"

"Not in so many words. But there was some discussion about an old building. An *escuela*. A school."

"The school's the drop point?" I wondered. "But that's right in the middle of town."

"Listen to you," Anthony said. "This isn't some silly novel. You need to stay out of this."

"You worry about protecting yourself," I said. "You don't need to worry about protecting me."

"Just promise me you won't get involved in this mess."

"I already have one man in my life telling me what to do. I don't need another."

"In case you haven't noticed," he said. "I'm not exactly in your life."

"Well, that's probably best now, isn't it?"

Anthony shut his mouth. His response flamed in his eyes.

29

A woman should never let a man make her miss lunch.

By the time I made it to the buffet table, all that remained was a plate of leftover fruit. I picked up a wedge of cantaloupe and ate it with defiance.

The rest of the group gathered. They looked annoyingly

well fed.

Shortly after, Hector arrived. He quickly dismissed us, telling us the afternoon tour had been cancelled. He instructed us to meet him in the lodge promptly at three o' clock for a cooking demonstration.

He left. I was overcome with an irrational need to know what he was up to. So I tailed him again.

I was damn lucky the man wasn't more observant.

He made a brief stop at an outbuilding and emerged with a backpack in his hands. He took the fork in the road that led to the rickety bridge where the driver of the minibus kicked us out on the first day.

I stayed out of sight by keeping to the edge of the vegetation. Hector veered off before he reached the bridge. It looked like he took off into the jungle, but when I reached the place where he'd turned off, I saw that a road — now overgrown — had once been there.

I slogged along, following Hector's trail. The sun had reached its peak around lunchtime and now was the hottest part of the day. The farther away from the lodge I followed Hector, the more the heat smothered.

It felt like someone had soaked a blanket in a tub and tossed it over my head. The heaviness of the wet air pressed down on the tops of my feet. It drooped my shoulders. It flattened my hair. Water trickled down my hairline. Sweat pooled in every dimple of my body.

Miserably, I wished for rain. The frequent showers over the past few days seemed to result from water coalescing straight out of the air rather than spilling from the sky above. For a brief time after each shower, there was a reprieve before the blanket of air started soaking again, surging towards the saturation point.

I fidgeted with my clothes. My shirt clung like a banana peel, my shorts rode up my thighs, my feet sloshed in my sandals. My bra was nothing short of torture.

Like legions of women before me, I secretly hated bras.

Ever since the day in junior high school when I announced to my mother that I had to wear one or else die a painful, shame-caused death in gym class.

Don't get me wrong, I always wore the damn things. I loathed nipplage and wigglage and droopage as much as any woman, but that didn't make the wiry, strappy, squishy things any more comfortable.

Especially not on a day like this.

I stopped. Hector snapped a twig somewhere in front of me, but I couldn't see him or anyone else. I looked around just to be sure.

My elbows and hands disappeared down my sleeves. I engaged in some hasty maneuvering until I was free of the beastly undergarment. I poked my arms back through my sleeves and shoved the bra in the pocket of my shorts.

I trudged onward. Soon, I was longing for a cold glass of lemonade or a frosty root beer or a long island iced tea or—

In my preoccupation, I failed to notice that Hector had stopped. He was turning towards me. I dove into a tangle of ropy vegetation, terrified that he'd discovered me. I watched him through the vines, waiting to see what he would do.

Hector swiveled back around, apparently convinced that he was alone. My vision blurred and I realized that I had stopped breathing. I gulped in huge mouthfuls of air and my vision cleared.

Hector entered a building that I had not noticed before. A little blue building exactly like the one in the village.

The *escuela*.

The area around the school had once been cleared. Judging from the width of the overgrown road we'd followed, I guessed that at one time, the town had been here. The villagers probably moved the site when the main road was put in.

Hector tucked the bag he'd been carrying inside the front door of the old school. Then he hurried back the way he'd come. I ducked deeper into my hiding place and it dawned on me that I had no idea what was supposed to happen next.

Anthony's translation had not revealed what time the swap was to occur. Surely Rosa wouldn't be left out here in the middle of nowhere. Was Luis expecting Rosa to find her own way home? Did he really trust the kidnapper to give the girl back once the money was retrieved?

Hector had instructed us to meet him at the lodge at three o' clock. Could that be when the swap was supposed to take place? Was he trying to make sure we stayed out of the way? If that was the case, it was too late for me. I was here. The question was — what was I going to do about that?

In the end, I decided it would be best for me to stay. That way, if Rosa was left here alone, I could take her home. And if the kidnapper didn't follow through — how trustworthy could a kidnapper be — then maybe I could take a few pictures. Collect evidence. That's what sleuths did.

Right?

Oh no. What if the kidnapper threatened to do unspeakable things to Rosa if someone was discovered at the drop point? Kidnappers always made threats like that in the movies. But then the good guys always ignored those threats and staked out the drop point anyway. Maybe it was different here. Maybe there was a weird code of honor.

Hector did say that here they take care of their own. But I was an outsider. I wouldn't be bound by the same code, would I?

Still, I didn't want to foul this up. I needed to be well hidden.

I crawled between the buttresses of a towering tree. I craned my neck back, but could not see the top. The colossal tree made me feel tiny and insignificant. A weird firing of my synapses made me think of the Eiffel Tower. Most people didn't know that the distinctive shape of the famous Paris landmark had nothing to do with art. The designer of the Eiffel Tower made it that way to resist the effects of wind.

Many tropical trees, like the one I was hiding under, used a similar design to keep from toppling. The soil was too shallow for an underground network of roots, so instead the roots flared out above the ground. These roots — known as buttresses — performed a function similar to the sprawling base of the Eiffel Tower.

As I knelt between them, the triangle-shaped buttresses soared above my head. They protected the tree from the wind. I hoped they would also protect me from the kidnapper.

I waited.

Time ticked by.

Just as I was wondering how long I would be willing to wait, the soft pad of footsteps sounded in the still air.

30

I didn't realize what a mistake I had made.

Since I had already used my camera three times that day — to review pictures from the raft trip and to record and replay the video of Luis and Hector — I was afraid the battery would die. So I kept the camera off.

That would turn out to be serious a mistake.

As I waited for something to happen, I burrowed down in my hiding place and reached out with my senses.

I wished for some kind of extra sensory perception. I had seen on TV that everyone possessed the ability to use ESP, but we had long since forgotten how to use it.

I thought the same thing was happening to regular sensory perception, our ability to see, hear, taste, smell, and touch. We'd become so distracted and lulled and desensitized to the world by technology and comfort that we'd forgotten how to use our senses.

Sights were dimmed by the glare of lights and smog, smells were smothered by the scent of perfume, tastes were muted by the processing of foods, sounds were drowned out by the din of machines, and rarely did we remember to reach out and touch one another.

Here it was different. Here everything was raw and natural and loud. That's what made the unexpected silence so noticeable.

The jungle was normally a cacophony of bugs and birds and howling monkeys. But as I focused my senses, the oppressive heat made the jungle drowsy and eerily quiet.

Behind a bright web of palm leaves, a shadow moved.
I turned my camera on.
The shadow drifted towards the schoolhouse.

I twisted the dial that controlled the camera's zoom. I wished I had thought to bring my other camera. The zoom on my SLR was much better. But if I had gone back to the room to get it, I wouldn't have been able to follow Hector. This was the best I could do.

The lens twirled out of the front of my camera. The movement made a faint whirring sound followed by a click.

The shadow paused.

I cursed the camera and I cursed myself and hoped the pause was a coincidence. The sound had not been that loud.

Unless the other person had been listening as hard as I was. I held my breath and waited. I watched the shadow. It was too indistinct to make out details of the person who created it.

The shadow vanished.

I slouched back into my hiding place and waited.

I stayed there until the mid-afternoon sun sent shadows creeping through the jungle. I jumped at each one, certain the mysterious visitor had come back. Then I crawled out of my hiding place and skulked back to the lodge, defeated.

I cowered at the bar.

When I had returned from my failed mission, I had gone back to the room to clean up. While I was there, I reached out to my camera gear for comfort.

I had lugged the bag with all its contents back to the lodge with me. I now pulled out my SLR and set it aside. I searched for the slim black case I had hidden beneath it.

Anthony found me. "You look lost in thought," he said. "Mind if I get lost with you?"

I clung to the case and didn't answer.

"You're going to tell me to get lost period, aren't you?"

I sighed. "No."

"Truce?"

"Truce."

"So what happened?" he asked.

"Who says anything happened?"

"You wouldn't promise me not to get involved, so I can only assume you got involved."

I held up the black case. "You ever use filters?"

"No," he said. "I prefer to see things as they are."

"My friend Kaylee gave me these." I flipped through the plastic sleeves that filled the case. Each one held a circle of glass.

"So what do filters have to do with you not getting involved?"

"I screwed up again."

"What do you mean again?"

Why was I telling him this?

Anthony waited for me to answer.

I had to say something. "I let her down."

"Who are you talking about? Kaylee or Rosa?"

I reached the last sleeve. I started flipping through them backwards.

"You did get involved, didn't you?"

I studied one of the filters.

"And it reminds you of something that happened with your friend."

"Kaylee gave me a filter every year for my birthday."

Anthony listened.

"She'd always tell me, *This year I want you to see the world a little differently.*" I removed the circle of glass from the sleeve and held it up. It was tinted a pale yellow. "This one's a warming filter. It was the first one Kaylee gave me. She said it would make the world brighter. Warmer. Cheerier."

I put the filter back. I slipped out another.

"This clear one is a polarizer. Kaylee said this was the most important filter I could own. She said it would make things clearer. She said it would make blue skies bluer." I put it back inside of the case.

Anthony watched as I flipped to the end of the book.

"This one—" I placed my thumb and forefinger on the edge of a filter and pulled it out. "This is the last one she gave me. It's a graduated neutral density filter." I held it up. "See how it's clear on one half and then gradually becomes darker and darker on the other half?"

"Yes."

"It balances the light in a scene."

"So the sky isn't washed out," he said. "Or the foreground too dark."

I twirled the filter in the late day light slanting into the lodge. "When Kaylee gave me this one, she told me, *Aurora, there are times when you need to see the light in the dark and other times when you need to see the dark in the light.*"

"What did she mean by that?"

"Hell if I know." I put the filter away. "I think she was foreshadowing."

"Foreshadowing what?"

"You were right, you know."

"No, I don't know. You've totally lost me."

"I did get involved." I zipped the case shut. "I scared away the kidnapper."

31

This was supposed to be a simple trip.

Fly to Costa Rica. Do a little rafting. Go on a couple of tours. Eat a lot of food. Write an article. Go home.

How did it manage to spiral so out of control?

My dad and I still weren't speaking. After the incident on the river, we exchanged a frantic *Are you all right?* and *Are you okay?* and *Are you sure?* and then lapsed back into an uneasy silence.

I ached for reconciliation, but the evil part of me blamed my dad for the flip-flop I took over the raft. If he hadn't held on to me, I might have been spared the image of my white legs flailing across the lodge wall.

But that was the least of my worries. I was also dancing on the edge of a relationship with a sexy archaeologist, I had nearly drowned in a river, and an innocent girl had gone missing. Worst of all, I might be the reason the girl had not yet come home.

What was I going to do about all of this? Where could I even start?

"This way." Anthony pointed down a trail that led into the tangled jungle. It appeared I would have to deal with the sexy archaeologist first.

I had confessed everything to him. About following Hector, about sneaking out to the old schoolhouse, about scaring away the kidnapper. I asked him if I should tell someone what I had done.

Anthony said he thought it was best to wait. He thought

the lure of the money would be too much to keep the kidnapper away. He thought Rosa would be back by morning.

I wasn't sure about any of this. But I decided to listen to his advice for now. If only the police had come. Maybe then I would have someone to tell.

For now, Anthony was determined to distract me again. I followed him down the trail. It led over a dark hill and into a valley. There, the jungle folded back to reveal a ribbon waterfall pouring long and thin into a blue-black pool.

"Wow," I said. "How did you find this?"

"I've been here a while. Did some exploring."

A ribbon of water curved over a nickpoint in the rock. The waning sunlight skittered off the water and ping-ponged around the clearing.

"Do you mind?" I held up my camera bag.

"Of course not."

Anthony watched as I composed several shots. I did not use a filter. I preferred to see it just as it was. "Thank you for showing me this."

"Con much gusto."

I lowered my camera. "I like it when you say that."

Anthony gave me an odd look.

I busied myself with resetting the aperture of my lens.

"Why do you do this?" he asked.

I looked up. "What?"

"This." He made a sweeping gesture that took in me, my camera, the jungle, all of Costa Rica. "What you do."

"Adventure travel?"

"Is that what you call it?"

"Sure."

"Okay, then. Adventure travel. Why do you do it?"

"You make it sound like I'm doing something illegal."

"You're not going to tell me."

"You'd think it's silly."

"Try me."

I propped myself on a rock. "When you were a kid, didn't you ever want to be a hero on an adventure? A fearless explorer? The star of your own movie?"

"What do you mean, want to be?" Anthony reclined on a rock a few feet away from me. "I am a hero."

"I told you you'd make fun of me."

"I'm just messing with you." He leaned back on one elbow. "I guess I thought only boys wanted to be big, bad super-heroes. I figured girls wanted to be brides or princesses."

I snorted. "Sure, but Princess Leia was a princess and a hero."

"You got me there. So, you want to be a hot, intergalactic traveler in a white bathrobe with cinnamon rolls glued to your head, is that it?"

"Forget it."

"Seriously."

I folded up the strap on my camera and tucked it back in my bag.

"Come on. I promise not to tease you."

I shot him a disbelieving look.

"Much."

I set the bag on the ground. "I guess a lot of it has to do with my mom. She's always been so brave, so gutsy. You'd probably say she's got a real set of granite spheres."

"Ah — a ballsy woman." Anthony said. "That explains a lot about you. I just figured you got that from your dad."

"No, after the divorce my mom raised us — I have a sister — she raised the two of us mostly on her own. We stayed with some friends for a while, but then my mom set out on her own. I always admired her for that."

"But?"

"Well — my mom always had to work hard and we never really got to go anywhere. So I would lay awake every night and dream of seeing strange lands, eating weird foods, meeting exotic people. I would lay awake and dream of finding something that made me feel, you know — alive."

"So have you?"

"Have I what?"

"Found what makes you feel alive."

"Oh — I don't know," I said. "It's just so easy to feel dead when you're surrounded by dead things. Refrigerators, computers, high heel shoes. Photos of long gone friends."

Anthony sobered.

"Sometimes I do, I guess. But it fades so quickly." I looked across the pool to where the ribbon fall tickled the surface of the water. Waves rippled out in every direction. "I keep thinking one day I'll say aha! This is it. This is me. This is where I belong. This is what makes me feel alive." I trailed my finger in the water, creating a series of counter waves. The opposing ripples collided in a mini natural disaster.

Anthony leaned forward. Rested an elbow on one knee.

"Honestly," I said. "Most of the time when I get out there, when I go some place new, I get scared. Like I'm going to mess up, trip over a cliff, walk into the wrong part of town."

"Drown in a river," he said.

"Yeah, exactly. I imagine myself as a fearless adventurer, but the truth is, I kind of stick to safe stuff like these group tours, and usually some part of me always wants to go home." I shook my head. "You must think I'm an idiot. I'm not making any sense."

He picked up a pebble and threw it in the water. It created another quiet calamity. "The safe thing would be to stay home and watch reality shows," he said.

I drew my knees up and propped my elbows on them.

Anthony spoke in a low voice. "I see you perfectly."

I looked up, startled. "How do you figure?"

"You're a collector." He tossed another pebble in the pool. "Some people collect things. Cars, electronics, clothes, high heel shoes. You collect experiences."

"Great. So I have been-there-done-that syndrome." I said. "Trips are my status symbols."

"Could be."

I rested my chin on my forearms.

"But I don't think it's that way for you," Anthony continued. "I've watched you."

I swiveled my head to the side. It made me feel funny to think of him watching me.

"You try to feel a place," he said. "Absorb it. Connect with it. That's what I like about you."

His words surprised me. I lifted my head and met his eyes.

He seemed so fully present, like nothing could possibly preoccupy his mind. His eyes held an intense awareness where in most people there was a vacancy, an emptiness, a disinterest, a wandering.

The only person I had ever known like that was Kaylee. Others in my life felt shaded to me, like I was trying to peer into their soul through the gauziness of a sheer curtain. Whatever it was that lighted their inner being was filtered, diffuse.

But with Anthony, his essence shone out with a dizzying brilliance. I wondered, did he make everyone feel this way? Or did I somehow ignite a brighter fire in him? Stoke some inner source of heat? Whatever the case, I enjoyed basking in the warmth. The look on his face at that moment was unreadable, but it hinted at a certain kind of longing.

Light glinted off the pool and into my eyes. I tried to reposition myself away from the brightness.

"Wait," Anthony said. He slid across the rocks towards me. He reached up and traced his thumb across my cheek. "The reflection off the water is making little waves on your face."

He ran a finger over my forehead. The pattern he traced almost made it possible for me to perceive the ripples of light.

I was completely unable to move.

Anthony leaned forward and brushed his lips across mine. "It's just the two of us out here."

I nearly wobbled off the rock. "Maybe," I said, "we should go back to the rooms."

32

The rooms were really a set of five bungalows connected by a shared patio. Now that I was staying with Stacy, my room was right next door to Anthony's.

As soon as we returned from our hike, I sent Anthony to his room before I could succumb to his decadent powers.

The hike had made me overheat in more ways than one, so I decided to take a shower. Then I figured maybe I would do some writing. I needed to keep busy so I wouldn't obsess about Rosa.

I stripped off my clothes and stepped into the bathroom. I could hardly wait to try out my new shampoo. I hoped it would make my hair as lovely as Grace's. I pulled back the shower curtain and reached in to turn on the water.

"Holyshit!"

I backed away from the shower, dove out of the bathroom, stumbled against the closet, pitched into the bedroom, tripped over my suitcase, fell on the floor, flailed my legs in the air, scrabbled to get back up, lunged towards the front door, and burst outside.

Anthony flew out of his room. "What happened? Are you all right?"

"No. No! I'm not all right. That damn alligator is curled up in the bottom of the shower."

"Alligator?" Anthony said. "What alligator?"

"The one that lives in the pond — Tico, remember?"

"Well now," Anthony said, "isn't this interesting?"

"Interesting? You call this interesting?"

"Remind me to thank him."

"Thank him?!" I snapped like an alligator, all white teeth and angry jaws. "What the hell're you talking about?"

He leaned against the door frame and folded his arms over his chest.

"Stop lolling around and do something!" I was getting a little shrieky.

"I'm thinking about it," he said.

"Well — what're you waiting for?"

"I'm afraid I'll get slapped."

"By an alligator?"

I noticed that Anthony was not looking at my room.

"Oh shit," I said. He was looking at me.

"You should watch your language."

"You shouldn't stare," I said.

"Am I em-bare-assing you again?"

"Bare assed? I'm completely goddam naked."

"It's kind of sexy when you cuss like that."

"Damn it, Anthony. Go in there and get my clothes."

"I'm not going in there. An alligator's in the shower. How did he get there, anyway?"

I made a frustrated growling noise. A small crowd started to gather. Anthony went into his room and came out with a sheet.

"Here," he said.

I wrapped myself up.

"Now what?" I asked.

"Wrestling gators isn't my specialty."

"Perfect."

"I would be happy to show you what my specialty is, though."

"I'm sure you would."

"Your room is occupied at the moment. We could go to mine."

"Will you shut up? Someone will hear you."

Eventually, Hector came along, slipped a noose over Tico's neck, dangled some dinner in front of his snout, and led him away.

"I owe that gator a beer," Anthony said. He looked me over. "No, make that a six-pack. And by the way, I'll be wanting that sheet back."

"In your dreams."

I went back into my room and dressed.
I decided to skip the shower.
It was full of caiman cooties.

33

What was I thinking, trying to do this now?

After the episode with Tico I didn't know what to do with myself, so I settled down to write.

A half hour later, I still stared at a blank sheet of paper. It was just too hard, what with everything that had been going on.

Tomorrow it would be much easier.

Tomorrow I would have had a better night's sleep. I would have gotten up earlier, perkier, probably even prettier from the refreshing night's sleep I'd had.

I would have exercised, eaten oatmeal for breakfast, and only had one cup of coffee instead of four. Instead of being jittery, overtired, and cranky, I would be wide-eyed, bright, and focused.

If I waited until tomorrow the muse would perch on my shoulder and whisper in my ear. The words would flow. I would write a Pulitzer-prize worthy article.

There would be plenty of time. After all, the article only had to be two thousand words. A cinch. If I went to sleep now, my subconscious brain would devise the perfect lead for the story during the night.

In fact, I would fall asleep faster and rest a lot more

soundly if I went to the lodge to unwind and have a drink. Just one. Maybe two. Definitely no more than two.

I needed to get my mind off all this work anyway. It was mucking up my creativity.

I took the lodge steps two at a time.

"Pura vida!"

The shout came from the bar. The college kids, Stacy included, were sampling some of the local beverages.

"Heyyyyy," one of the guys slurred. "You gotta try this shtuff. It's the national drink. Guaro, ish that what they call it? Like tequila in Mexico or vodka in Russia or—" He lost his train of thought.

I wondered if the four kids were even of drinking age. Then I wondered when I had gotten so old.

I glanced around the lodge, hoping to find Anthony.

In a dark corner, the newlyweds cuddled together. Near the kitchen, Hector and Grace chatted. At the bar, my dad pulled up a stool, getting ready to join the fun. Stacy handed him the bottle of Guaro. Then she tossed back a shot. I was glad Tarzan wasn't there hanging all over her.

I did not find Anthony.

The scene didn't appeal to me, so I changed my mind about the drink, went back to my room, and stumbled into bed.

I'm writing!

I actually got up early and started writing.

It's going great. I knew it would be easy. My laptop isn't here, so I absolutely can't get sidetracked by checking e-mail or doing research on the internet. I'm on a roll!

Hmmm. Time for a break.

I think I'll count how many words I've written. I want to see out how far I've gotten on my article. Look at that. Two-hundred-and-fifty words. This is great! I'm already an eighth of the way there. What should I write next?

It'll come to me.

In a minute.

Well — maybe I'll read what I already have. That'll get me going again. I know it'll be perfect, no revision necessary.

Oh. That first sentence isn't that great. Well, maybe I'll use my pocket thesaurus to find a better word.

There. That's better.

Hmm. The second sentence is going to need a little work, too. Maybe I'll just push on and read the whole thing. The rest will be great. I know it. After all, the first couple sentences are just for warming up, right?

Oh no. It all sucks. I can't use any of this. What was I thinking, anyway? I'll never be a great writer. Great writers always create masterpieces.

Wait, I know what the problem is.

I only had one cup of coffee this morning, made in the crappy coffee pot in the room. I bet if I go to the lodge and drink a few cups of real coffee, my brain cells will function much better. I mean, I've deprived them of their normal dose of caffeine. That'd muck up anyone's creativity, right?

I went to the lodge and sucked down three cups of coffee.

I got the jitters. I fretted about Rosa. It was eight in the morning. If she'd been returned in the night, I would have heard something by now.

No one else was in the lodge. Stacy had passed out in the room sometime after midnight. If her condition was any indication, I wouldn't be seeing any of the others for a while.

I decided to go to the village and find out what was going on.

Twenty minutes later I positioned myself before Luis's front door. At first there wasn't any activity, but then a baby wailed. I drew up to my full five-foot-two, gathered my courage, stepped forward, and rapped on the door.

Luis answered. "Aurora Night," he said.

"Listen — I have to talk to you. I need to tell you something."

Luis motioned for me to come inside.

"Have you found out anything about Rosa?" I asked.

"No. I left the money, but he not come. I took it away this morning."

I was stunned. I wanted to shake him. I wanted to ask him why he didn't leave the money longer, why he didn't call the police, why he didn't do more to find his daughter.

Usually, I don't feel like shaking people. Must be the coffee.

The woman and the baby I had seen before entered the room.

"This is my wife," Luis said. "She not speak English."

The woman exuded pride and strength, but her eyes suggested something different. Worry. Sleepless nights.

My whole body clenched with guilt. "Luis—"

"You like to hold the baby?" he asked.

"Oh, I — I don't know."

"Here." He took the baby from his wife and handed it to me. "A boy."

I bounced the baby on my hip. I felt the strange mix of emotions that always hit me when I held a baby. A swirl of fear and longing. I always thought that someday I might want a baby of my own, but my current lifestyle didn't exactly lend itself to motherhood. I didn't think people would look kindly on me strapping a Baby Björn to my chest and climbing in a raft.

I handed the baby boy to his mother. "Gracias," I said.

She laid the infant in a cradle. He closed his eyes, tilted his head to the side, and put his arms up in complete surrender to the comforts of bed and family. His hands curled into balls like he was clutching something precious.

I turned to Luis. "About Rosa—"

"My niña," he said. He looked down at his son and ran a finger over the baby's face. "Her cheek, so soft when I kiss her good night." Luis's voice caught. "I so much miss her."

I lowered my gaze.

How did anyone handle being a parent? The world was positively rife with peril. Every stranger shadowing the front door, every pot boiling on the stove, every virus worming its way around the planet, every car speeding down the highway must seem an ominous threat.

A twinge of regret pulsed through my veins. I realized that a father with a daughter, whether she's nine or twenty-nine, is a man afraid.

"It's my fault the kidnapper didn't take the money," I said at last. I told Luis everything. "You see? It's my fault."

"No," he said. "I should have called the police. I do it now. Several hours it will take for them to come from Golfito. They will wish to speak with you."

"Of course." I excused myself and left the house. I felt relieved and sick at the same time.

Luis had gallantly shouldered the blame.

I knew better.

34

"What're you doing?" Stacy asked.

"Thinking."

"You're always thinking. You need to have a little fun on this trip if you're going to write a decent article."

"Who says I'm not having any fun?"

"Well, for one thing, Mr. Ripped's been panting after you like a dog in heat, and you're not doing anything about it."

"Thanks for the nice image."

"Oh! I've been meaning to tell you, it was SO romantic the way he saved your life."

I didn't reply.

Stacy didn't notice. "Anthony practically went to blows with Tarzan to make him stop the raft so he could get out and save you."

"That was dangerous and stupid."

"That's why it was so romantic."

"Maybe in your warped world."

"It gets better. Anthony argued with your dad, too. Over who would rescue you."

"My dad?"

"I was thinking — that's just the thing for *Ripped Night*. The sexy hero saves the damsel in distress."

I groaned. That's all I needed. A vapid romance heroine based on me. I felt like screaming at Stacy, "That's not who I want to be!" If I had to be a romantic heroine, I wanted to be like Princess Leia. She managed to be sexy and funny and irresistible by acting bossy and haughty and keeping Han Solo guessing all the time.

"You need to relax," Stacy said. "Like me. I have an appointment at the spa this afternoon."

"I went to the spa, too, you know."

"Yeah, but I bet you stressed out the whole time."

"Did not." Damn it. The girl knew me too well.

"Right now, I'm going on the nature hike," she said. "You should come. Hector's leading it." She winked.

"You really think he's cute, huh?"

"Sure. Now do me a favor. Stop wallowing and find something — or someone — fun to do. You always put too much pressure on yourself." Stacy breezed out of the room.

She left me all alone with my thoughts. Too much pressure she'd said. That might be the word that defined an entire generation of women. Pressure.

The female sex has always been under a lot of pressure, but these days, the pressure we heap on ourselves might be worst of all.

It used to be, the only thing a woman had to pressure herself about was whether her cooking was as good as her mother-in-law's or if her dress was as nice as the neighbor's. Then TV came along and a woman had to compare herself to Beaver Cleaver's mom and the models that sold dish washing soap.

By the time I reached adulthood, TV had it that a woman was supposed to roll out of bed at o'dark-thirty, nurse the Gerber baby, pump a day's worth of breast milk, dash off to her Tae Kwon Do class, spar with her adonis instructor, dress in a tight business suit and stiletto heels, go to her high-powered law job, win a case by noon, meet a mysterious informant during lunch, when naturally, everything would go wrong and she would be forced to kick some ass, then go back to court with nary a hair out of place, win another case, go home and prepare a delicious four-course meal for studly husband, nurse Gerber baby into instant angelic sleep, transform into sex goddess, and crawl into a set of perfectly pressed silk sheets wearing a negligee she fit into at her pre-wedding lingerie party.

And if she was lucky, she wouldn't get a call in the middle of the night telling her to go kick some more ass.

That was just TV.

In the movies, ninety-pound Princess Leia overpowered two-ton Jabba the Hut with the chain that imprisoned her before rescuing her friends from the gaping jaws of the terrible man-eating monster in the ground.

All while dressed as a pole-dancer.

And, of course, my personal favorite, waitress turned terminator-killer, Sarah Connor who looked amazing dressed in a slinky black tank top with coordinating combat gear.

How I longed to be her.

Maybe Stacy had a point. Perhaps my need for adventure and my need to save the day were making me put too much pressure on myself.

I pulled out the trip itinerary. The nature hike she mentioned led to another waterfall.

Stacy was right, I needed to get out. And since I wasn't planning on doing somebody, that left doing something.

I guess the hike started out well enough.

"You decided to come!" Stacy bounded over to me and hugged me like a long lost friend. Hector stood nearby. He must have been the reason for her nervous flutter.

"Of course," I said. "I couldn't miss watching you crash

and burn."

"Ouch," she said. "Check out who else is joining us."

Anthony swung up the steps.

Despite Stacy's advice to have more fun, I planned to get some work done on this hike. I wanted to take notes and shoot some pictures. Because of the magazine's publication cycle, our article was due two days after my dad and I got home. I was feeling pressed for time.

I didn't need Anthony complicating things.

The newlyweds decided to stay behind. The rest of us joined Hector for the hike. He led us down yet another of the area's many trails. The path snaked away from the lodge and slithered out into the jungle.

As soon as we were away from the lodge, a flash of yellow and black caught our attention.

Video-camera-kid flipped on his camera. I resented how he always had the dang thing with him. I still hadn't forgiven him for plastering my white legs across the lodge's wall.

The kid studied the image on his screen. "Hey," he said. "Isn't that the cereal bird?"

Stacy whapped him on the back of the head. "You're the fruit loop, idiot. That happens to be a toucan." She looked at Hector to see if he was impressed.

Video-camera-kid zoomed in. "Will you get a load of the schnoz on that thing? His nose is bigger than his body."

We pondered the bird's giant nose. It looked like a dreadful burden to carry.

"A toucan's beak," Hector said, "is actually a third of the bird's total body length. If you consider the toucan's entire surface area, the beak is closer to forty percent."

Stacy leaned in to Hector. "So why," she said, "does the bird have such a big appendage?"

"The toucan's beak is large because of the heat," Hector said. "I once saw an infrared photo of a toucan. The bird's body showed up as blue in the image, but the beak glowed with yellow and red. This is because the toucan's beak acts like a radiator. When the bird is hot, blood rushes to the beak and transfers heat into the air."

The group moved on. I lingered behind to take a picture.

The toucan took one look at me and flew away.

Frustrated, I hastened to catch up. I wouldn't have been in such a hurry if I knew what waited around the next bend.

Hector stopped before the bend in the trail and waited for us to catch up. He opened his mouth to say something, but Stacy interrupted.

"Will you tell us," she said, "why Costa Ricans are called Ticos?"

Hector appeared annoyed by the interruption, but he answered her question. "Tico is a symbol of our democracy and equality. Many of our people believe we are all *hermanticos*, or little brothers. Others say it is because we add tico, which means little, to the end of many words. For example, *momentico*, which means a little moment. In this case, Tico is a symbol of the friendliness of our people."

Stacy crinkled her forehead. "No offense," she said, "but not every Tico is friendly. Our bus driver the other day sure as heck wasn't."

"This is a problem of the cities," Hector said. "They teach our people to live apart. It is my belief that the number one threat facing our country is the breakdown of the community, of the family. My parents moved to the city. Everyday, I worry for them."

"See that?" Stacy whispered to me. "He's so sweet. He worries about his mom and dad."

I looked at my own dad and remembered how I had treated him. I sure as heck wasn't very sweet.

We rounded the bend in the trail.

The path spilled over a sheer rock wall and descended straight down.

"Eighty vertical feet," Hector said, pointing to the bottom. "We go this way."

35

A thousand places to see before I die? It was more like a thousand places to make me die.

I swayed as I peered over the wall. A ledge, the width of a slice of bread, angled down the side. A tight cable hovered above the ledge. To make it to the bottom, we needed to creep along the ledge, between the wall and the cable.

Talk about a rock and a hard place.

Hector went first. Then Stacy, me, Anthony, and the rest of the group. I gripped the wall with one hand and the cable with the other. I tried not to look down.

Hector and Stacy moved ahead with the ease of mountain goats. Hector stopped to watch our progress. "You are okay?" he asked.

I guess my terror was noticeable.

"Sure," I said, with more confidence than I felt. "You know — considering how small your country is, it sure is full of surprises."

"My country is bigger than you think," Hector said. "Many times it has been compared to your state of West Virginia. This is not true." He turned and continued along the wall.

I made the mistake of looking down. I saw nothing but empty air. A long line of people pressed at my back, so there was no way I could turn around. I inched forward to where Hector waited.

"Why do you say that's not true?" I asked him. "About West Virginia?"

"Maybe if you measure mile by mile," he said, "the size is the same. But if you measure other ways, you will find our country is as vast as your United States."

"Oh, really. How so?"

"Like your country, we have an Atlantic Coast, different from our Pacific coast. We have a continental divide that splits us in two, like your Rocky Mountains. Volcanoes erupt over our towns, crops fill our central plains, urban problems take over our cities. Even our histories are similar. European conquest, colonization, independence, civil war, industrialization. Sound familiar?" Hector moved on.

I swayed uneasily and closed my eyes.

"Breathe," Anthony said against my hair. His sudden closeness made me quiver.

I opened my eyes and inched forward.

"That's a girl," Anthony said.

Hector continued to talk as he sauntered down the cliff. "Your country is a crossroads between the east and west. It connects the world to make it round. Here, we are an isthmus, a land bridge, a crossroads between the north and south."

My foot touched a mossy section of the rock. I slipped.

Anthony caught me at the waist. "Careful," he said, "it's slippery."

"No kidding?" I didn't mean to be sarcastic, but the last thing I needed to do was make a fool of myself again.

The group fell silent as we traversed another thirty feet of slimy rock. The path ended in a wide ledge suspended above the ground. A staircase, green and slick from the soggy air, led the rest of the way down.

"So you see—" Hector spoke as though we were in a cushy conference room rather than dangling on the side of a rock face. "Comparing our country to a state so small diminishes who we are. Our mountains are three times as high, our roads twice as slow. We have more rain, more rivers, more kinds of animals, more types of plants. Our spirit is bigger."

"That," I said, "is what makes your country remarkable. Such a great size is contained in such a small space."

Hector looked at me as though noticing me for the first time. "You understand me," he said.

"I believe I do."

"We will see," he said.

"See what?"

"If you can write it right." Hector strode across the ledge and took the slippery stairs, two at a time, to the bottom.

I stood still, staring after him.

Anthony came up behind me. "Did he say something that upset you?"

"No," I said. "No, I'm fine." I crossed the ledge to the stairs and made my way down. What I told Anthony wasn't true. Hector did say something that upset me.

Write it right.

I took his words as a challenge. And as an admonition.

Those three little words gave voice to a conflict I struggled with every time I picked up a pen. Writing about the world's places was, for me, an enormous responsibility.

Many of the people who read *See!* would not believe the U.S. could be boiled down to five pictures and two-thousand words in a magazine article, but they'd accept this was true for pretty much any other place on the planet.

An entire nation, an entire people, an entire culture was often reduced to a single image, a single phrase, a single word.

Every time I wrote, I was aware the choices I made could profoundly affect a reader's perception of a place. Eco-paradise, outdoor recreation mecca, third-world country, overgrown jungle, overgrown city.

Depending on the slant I chose, a few artfully arranged photos, and a handful of carefully selected words, I could forever paint a picture in people's minds of a place they might never see.

Sometimes the enormous responsibility I felt in writing about places overwhelmed me. Costa Rica was neither a war-torn, poverty-stricken country, nor a place where everyone lived the pura vida — pure life — touted by T-shirts and tourism websites.

Costa Rica is and has been all of these things, even as the U.S. is and has. Spending a week in Costa Rica would not make me an expert on its culture. But then again, spending a lifetime in the U.S. had not made me one either.

All I could do was write what I saw, in the best way I could. In that way, I suppose, the name of the magazine I worked for was just right. This is what I see. Now go see what you see.

Hector could not have known the effect his words would have on me.

I met him at the bottom and waited for the rest of the group to struggle off the wall. My dad joined us. I was afraid he'd picked that moment to try and patch things up.

I was wrong.

He had come to ask Hector a question. "There is one big difference between our countries," my dad said.

"And what is that?"

"You don't have a military. Doesn't that bother you? Aren't you worried about who will keep you safe?"

Hector picked up a leaf that littered the trail. He rolled the stem between his thumb and forefinger. "In the nineteen-eighties, some people in your country tried to fund military activities here in Costa Rica against the Sandinistas in Nicaragua."

"I remember that." my dad said. "The Contra scandal."

"Most in our country were not happy about this. So we elected a new president, Oscar Arias. He stopped the Contra activity here and developed a peace plan for all Central America. In time, the Sandinistas were ousted—" Hector tossed the leaf aside. "In a peaceful, democratic election."

"And Arias won the Nobel Peace Prize," my dad said.

"Yes," Hector said. "I am impressed."

My dad puffed up his chest.

"Usually," Hector said, "no one thinks of the good things about Central America. Only the drugs, the violence, the natural disasters."

"Don't forget the beer," my dad said.

"Ah, yes," Hector said. "To answer your question — No, it does not concern me. For Ticos, schools are our best defense."

Now that we were off the wall, the tensions that arose during our descent loosened. Together, we strolled beneath a vaulted ceiling of trees. A soft, misty light floated down like sunbeams drifting through a cathedral.

"This is the rainforest proper," Hector said. "The thick, tangled jungle only forms at the edge of the forest. Here, too little light comes through the canopy, so most of the undergrowth dies."

As we descended farther into the dimly lit archway of trees, the air around us took on a hushed, crypt-like quality. The only sound was the distant drone of a waterfall — the object of our journey.

We walked on until, at last, we rounded a bend and beheld the fall. Unlike the ribbon of water Anthony and I had seen earlier, this waterfall thundered over the side of the eighty-foot rock wall and crashed into a frothy bowl of foam.

Anthony took my hand in his. He laced his fingers through mine.

My heart skipped so many beats, I feared I might faint. I guess there must be something gooey and romantic about waterfalls.

Hector waded out into the white spray. The water came up to his knees. He beckoned for us to follow.

Anthony tugged at my hand "Are you coming?"

"In a minute." I unlaced my fingers from his and fished a plastic bag out of my pack. I wrapped it around my camera, leaving only the lens cap exposed.

I waded out to the fall with Anthony. As we drew nearer, tiny pellets of water pricked my skin.

Anthony grinned down at me. "My little water sprite."

I laughed and yelled back at him, "I'm not yours!"

I pulled the cap off my camera. I framed a shot looking out from the waterfall. Drops of water beaded across the lens. I pressed the shutter and captured an image of swirling water and light.

I adjusted the focus and pressed the shutter again. Then I shifted the view and framed another shot.

A smudge of red caught my eye.

I zoomed in. The camera's autofocus struggled to clarify the smeared image. I focused manually and slowly, the image began to resolve. The smudge of red transformed into a paddle.

Through the pebbly sound of the water, I heard a scream.

36

My first mistake was looking up.

But Stacy was pointing above my head. So I whirled and looked up.

Arms and legs and knees and elbows and flying yellow hair tumbled towards me.

My second mistake was not moving fast enough.

I lunged to the side, but the water dragged at my legs and slowed my escape. Something hit my hip hard and I went under.

I twisted in the water in a desperate attempt to keep my hand and my camera above the surface.

Dead weight pinned my legs on the bottom of the pool. I struggled with my free arm to propel myself to the surface. The dead weight held me in place.

Dead weight.

Dead.

The person trapping my legs was dead. Panic rose out of me like the bubbles of air escaping from my nose and mouth. I thrashed like a lunatic.

My camera vanished. Strong hands circled under my arms and tugged me free. My head was above water and I could breathe. But I continued to thrash in my need to escape death.

"Settle down." Anthony's voice broke through the drumming of the fall and the beating of my limbs against the water. "I've got you. You're okay."

He set me on the bank. Despite the heat, I shivered like a child caught in a snowstorm. I watched my dad and the others pull the body from the water.

"It's Tarzan, isn't it?" I said through chattering teeth. "He's dead, isn't he?"

Stacy sat beside me and smoothed the wet hair off my cheek. She held my camera. "Are you all right?" she asked.

"No." I watched as my dad and the others laid Tarzan gently on the bank. They attempted to do CPR.

After a moment, my dad rocked back on his heels. "It's too late," he said. "I think he's been dead a while."

I lurched up from my spot on the bank and rushed off to retch behind a tree. I steadied myself against the trunk and pressed my cheek to the bark. Its rough bite on my skin gave me something to focus on as I drew in deep breaths and strove to control my shaking.

I had never seen a dead body before. Not like this.

I had certainly never touched one. Waves of nausea shook me again. I closed my eyes and forced myself to calm down.

In my whole life, I'd had exactly three experiences with dead bodies — the funerals of three of my grandparents. My fourth grandparent, my dad's mother, chose to be cremated. Kaylee, too.

In my opinion, that was the more dignified way to go. I had never understood the custom of laying out the dead for others to gawk at. That was not the last image I wanted my loved ones to have of me.

When my grandparents passed, I was in my late teens, certainly old enough to go up to their caskets and pay my respects. But my parents had thankfully not pressed the issue when I said I didn't want to get that close. Now I had been so close, a dead body had plopped on top of me.

I shuddered one last time and prepared myself to face whatever happened next.

My dad and the three college boys stayed to watch over the body. The rest of us hiked out.

At the trailhead, we split up. Anthony and Hector went to the village to make arrangements for Tarzan's body. Stacy and I went back to the room.

I decided that having dead guy cooties on me was far worse than caiman cooties, so I took a long, hot shower.

I went to the lodge to wait for the others to return. Now that the adrenaline had drained away, I felt like I was coming down off a sugar and caffeine high from a triple espresso mocha frappacino with extra whipped cream. I felt queasy, my muscles hung limply, and tiredness settled behind my eyes.

I needed something to do, so I took out my camera — it was still in the plastic bag — and inspected it. The lens cap was lost. It had been in my hand and was now most likely at the bottom of the pool.

I took a cloth napkin from one of the tables and cleaned the water spots off the lens. Dampness lingered around the dial that controlled the f-stop, but the camera body worked fine and the lens would be okay once it dried. I set it on the table to air out. In this humidity, it took forever for anything to dry.

Anthony returned.

"What happened?" I asked him.

He sat in the chair across from me. "There were police in the village. Luis had called them about Rosa. They helped us gather some ropes and things to make a stretcher. It took all of us to get his body up the wall. We carried him as far as the lower ledge, then made a pulley to haul him the rest of the way up. The police asked a few questions, then left with the body for Golfito. They'll be back tomorrow to investigate."

"Do you think Tarzan was murdered?"

"Where'd you get that idea?" Anthony said. "We found a paddle in the water. The kind of paddle kayakers use. He probably had an accident and his body washed over the fall. The police think he died from a hit on the head. A rock, most likely."

"Oh," I said, not sure I believed it.

"They're setting out dinner," Anthony said. "You need to eat."

I poked my way through the line and put a few things on my plate, but I really wasn't hungry. Something was bothering me.

The other day on the river when the men fell into the hole, I had prioritized my dad's life and Anthony's life over Tarzan's. Now I couldn't help but wonder — was that the same as wishing him dead?

37

*D*ead body cooties didn't affect Anthony's appetite.

While I picked at my dinner, he devoured two plates of food. When he finished, he leaned back and surveyed the table. "You didn't eat much," he said.

"Not hungry."

"Is your camera all right?" he asked.

"It'll be okay."

"Bring it with you."

"Where?"

Anthony stacked the plates.

I followed him out of the lodge. Together, we trudged down the road that led to the village.

"Where are you taking me?" I asked.

"Trust me, will you?" He stopped beside a beat-up blue car parked in a small clearing.

"I'm supposed to trust you to drive me somewhere in that?"

"Get in," Anthony said. "It'll be worth it."

"What did you pay — five dollars — for this car?"

"Ten. Now shut up and get in. Or we're going to miss it."

"Miss what?"

Anthony didn't answer.

I lowered myself into the passenger's side. "You know, not long after you distracted me the last time, a body fell on me."

Anthony positioned himself on the driver's side. "It'll be hard to top that now, won't it?"

"You see the parallels, don't you? Nice hike. Pretty fall in the middle of the jungle—"

"Remember, the second waterfall was in a rainforest."

It felt wrong to treat Tarzan's death with lighthearted banter, but I supposed it functioned as a sort of coping mechanism.

"Where are we going?" I asked.

"It's not where. More like when."

Anthony drove a little ways then parked on a hill and checked his watch. We climbed out of the car and drifted to an overlook. As we stood there, our camera bags touching, a remarkable change began to occur.

"See that?" Anthony said, pleased. "The sweet light."

I had never met a man who knew of the sweet light, much less sought it out for me. "You do know photography."

"I know enough," he said. "I love this time of day. It's like someone shut off the glaring overhead lights and set a million candles ablaze. For just a moment, everything—trees, rocks, your hair—" He reached out and touched a lock. "Glows."

"Amazing."

Anthony dropped his hand and shifted his eyes.

"You're describing it exactly as I would," I said. "Only I never have."

"Twice every day," he said. "It's just a flash. So easy to

miss. Look, it's already fading. The sun sets so fast here. You didn't even get a picture."

"I always miss it in the morning. I know photographers are supposed to be early risers, catch the sunrise, the sweet light. But I like to sleep in too much."

"The evening light's better anyway," he said. "In the morning it's too damn cheery. Late in the day, it's more relaxed, mellow."

"Yeah, the light and me — we don't get along in the morning."

The lingering sweet light tinged the ends of Anthony's hair with red. He leaned closer until his face was a few inches from mine. "Have you seen the sweet light," he said, "when it makes everything drain of color?" His voice was lower now. Thicker, huskier. "It's— How do I describe it? Surreal. As if the world was dissolving. Like at the end of a movie."

Around us, the light grew dull.

"It passes," I said.

"Then it's like it always was."

"Or like it never happened."

"Wow," he said.

"Wow what?"

"For a minute there, I thought you were mocking me. Or at the very least you were thinking what an idiot I am."

"You are an idiot," I said.

Anthony swept in and kissed me just below my ear, on the ticklish part of my neck.

I squirmed. "You know what?" I said. "My dad used to pick me up at my mom's house for weekend visits when I was a kid. It was a long drive through the desert to his house. He would entertain me by telling me stories about alternate universes. If we drove a long time without seeing any headlights, he made me believe we were slipping into another reality. Then bump! we'd hit a crack in the road or a rock or a reflector light and get jarred back into our own dimension. I ate that stuff up. So no, I won't make fun of you for finding the light surreal."

"Careful," Anthony said. "I might get to know you."

"I was babbling."

"You were."

"Thanks."

"I like that I make you nervous."

"I didn't say—"

"In fact, while we're at it, tell me what happened to Kaylee."

"For god's sake, Anthony. That's none of your business."

"She's dead isn't she?"

I wrapped my arms around myself and looked at my feet. Nobody could accuse him of not being direct.

"Tell me," he said, gentler this time. "What happened?"

I don't know what made me say it. "She killed herself."

We didn't speak for a long time.

The jungle accepted the quiet of night. A dark shroud settled over us. The silence around us gathered strength, becoming a powerful motivator.

It compelled me to say more.

"Kaylee and me — we had this running joke," I said. "She was an investigative journalist and I'd tease her by saying that everything she wrote was too damn depressing. Then she'd say all I knew how to write were fluff pieces."

I breathed in the humid air.

"One day, about a year ago, Kaylee left for her last assignment. It ended up being longer than most. She was gone for months. When she came back, I didn't know, I thought things were the same." I looked up at the trees and watched the branches and leaves lose their definition in the encroaching darkness.

"We got together one night. She told me what happened over there. And still, I didn't know. Later that night, she e-mailed her story to her editor, then she—" I looked at Anthony for the first time since talking about Kaylee. "I was the last person to see her alive. All I could think is that I should have seen it. A sign, something."

"She didn't want you to know," he said.

"Yeah, well." I said. "I should have."

38

Someone had upped the stakes.

Tarzan was dead. And he had been my chief suspect in Rosa's disappearance.

I brooded over breakfast. Some hero I turned out to be. The day before I had dissolved into a useless, flubbering mess just because one little body fell on me. Okay, maybe not so little, but that wasn't the point.

I woke that morning with renewed determination in my quest to find Rosa. The problem was, with Tarzan dead, I was fresh out of ideas.

Anthony plopped a plate down across from me. He swung his leg over the back of the chair. "What's on your agenda today?" he asked.

I didn't want to tell him what I was thinking of doing, so I was evasive. "I don't know. This morning we're supposed to go on a canopy tour, but I'm thinking that's not such a good idea."

"Why not?"

"Have you noticed a pattern in my luck the past few days? Something tells me that attaching myself to a thin cable and zipping up and down the rainforest canopy is a bad idea."

"But zipline tours are practically synonymous with Costa Rica," he said. "You can't come all the way here and then miss out. Think of all the amazing habitats you could discover."

What he said was true. Entire worlds existed right above our heads. The canopy tours were the only way to access these delicate places, but I had a knot in my gut that told me this wasn't the time.

I changed the subject. "What're you doing today?"

Anthony finished chewing a mouthful of food and made a face. "Part of the deal with my university for taking a leave of absence is that I have to send in bi-monthly reports. That way they can keep track of the research I'm doing."

"Paperwork. Sounds fun. I think I'm going to do the same. I'd like to conduct some interviews and start compiling my notes."

What I didn't say was that I hoped to ferret out a clue to Rosa's whereabouts.

"All right then," Anthony said. "Sounds like you have a lot to do. I won't keep you." He inhaled the last of his breakfast and left.

I squared my shoulders and headed for the kitchen. Grace had gone in there earlier. I figured she was as good a choice as any to start my investigation. I hoped the police wouldn't get wind of what I was doing. I didn't want to get in trouble.

I stepped hesitantly into the kitchen, afraid of intruding on the busy cook staff.

Grace worked over a small bowl, scooping flour into it with a metal cup. A light powder fluffed into the air every time she dumped in another mound. The white dust settled over her black hair, which hung in a ropy braid over one shoulder.

"Are you busy?" I asked. That was a dumb question.

She used the back of her hand to brush back a stray wisp of hair. "How can I help you?"

"I was wondering if I could ask you some questions."

Grace considered the bowl before her.

"Just a couple," I added hastily. "For my article. If it's not a good time—"

"No, that is okay. Do you mind if I work while we talk? We are short staffed today."

Grace obviously took managing the lodge very seriously. She was willing to roll up her sleeves and dive into the flour when something needed to be done.

"Of course I don't mind," I said.

"What is your question?"

I inhaled and tried to speak, but the words hung in my throat. What was my question? I hadn't thought this through. I realized I was going to have to come clean.

"Um — I wasn't honest with you. What I really want to ask you about is Rosa."

Grace's eyebrows went up.

"About the ransom. I've been wondering, well — I've been to Luis's house. It's modest, to say the least. I can't figure out where he got the money to pay the ransom."

"He paid the money?" Grace asked.

"Well — I think he intended to."

"I see."

This was not going well. Why didn't I think this through first? I felt stuck, so I did the only logical thing and changed the subject. "What're you making there?" I asked.

"A white cake. It is for a dessert called tres leches, which means three milks. After I bake the cake, just before I serve it, I will pierce the top in many places, then I will pour condensed milk, evaporated milk, and eggnog over the top. The holes will allow the milk to penetrate the cake. This dessert is very traditional. We serve it with dollops of whip cream."

"Wow. Sounds delicious."

"At lunch you can try it. You will see. Now, about the money. Everyone here knows that Luis, along with many others, sold land to the national park."

"He did? How long ago was that?"

"A few months. I do not know the details. I was out of town visiting my sister, I think. The government had authority to designate Piedras Blancas as a park, but they could not force people to give up their land. It had to be bought at fair market price. And only if the owners agreed."

As Grace spoke, she cracked open several eggs and separated the whites into a large bowl. Now she turned on an electric mixer and beat the egg whites until stiff peaks formed.

I waited for her to shut off the mixer before I spoke. "Does the government pay for the land?"

"No." Grace folded in the yolks. "The money comes from the fundraising efforts of various conservation groups here and abroad. This is all I know." Grace stirred in the measured flour and then spooned in baking powder, sugar, and vanilla.

"I suppose," she said, "that you could talk to others who sold land to the park. Hector's parents, for instance, but no — they live in San José now." She tapped the handle of the spoon on the edge of the bowl. "There is someone else—"

A clatter at the back of the kitchen drew our attention.

"Excuse me." Grace wiped her hands on a towel and went to investigate.

I stayed where I was. The creamy smell of the cake batter made my eyes glaze over with desire. I couldn't wait for lunch. I was desperate to taste the tres leches.

Grace barked a few orders in Spanish, then she came back to the bowl.

"I am sorry," she said. "A cook dropped an entire bowl of rice. Now we will not have enough for lunch."

"With that dessert," I said. "I don't think anyone will care."

"You are probably right." Grace relaxed her shoulders. "The person you must speak to is don Pedro. He is a respected elder in our community. But, watch out. He will want to impress a pretty young woman."

39

I lied to the rest of the tour group.

I told them I wasn't going on the canopy tour because I had a headache. Since they'd witnessed a dead body plunk down on top of me, they didn't press the issue.

I waited until they left, then I set off for don Pedro's using the directions Grace had given me.

On the way, I couldn't help but feel bad for Luis. The poor man had sold all he had. He probably intended to use the money to build his family a new home or send his children to college.

Now, someone was trying to take it from him.

When I found don Pedro, if he hadn't been holding a metal pail in his hand, I would have thought he was on his way to a dance.

"Señorita," he said. A broad smile crinkled his caramel-colored skin. He tipped his cowboy hat and smoothed his neatly-pressed western-style shirt. His jeans crackled and his boots glinted as he strode forward and proffered a hand. As we exchanged greetings, I noticed the way his silver hair curled from under his hat and set off the light in his eyes.

I introduced myself and explained who sent me.

"Ah," he said. "Grace. She is a looker." He winked. "Also a fine business woman."

"If you're not too busy," I said, gesturing at the pail, "I'd like to ask you a few questions."

"Por favor." He held up a hand, indicating that I should

accompany him. "I am on my way to feed Gallo and Pinto." He rattled the bucket and showed me the golden grains inside.

I followed don Pedro down a path that led to a sagging barn. A crude fence wrapped around a muddied pen. Pock marks left by large hooves formed cups for little pools of rainwater.

Don Pedro shook the bucket. Two beasts lumbered out of the barn.

"Ox?" I asked. "Or is it oxen?"

"Oxen for two," don Pedro said.

The animals thrust their heads over the fence and reached for the bucket with their dexterous upper lips.

"Would you like to feed them?" Don Pedro held up the bucket.

"Oh, I don't know."

"They are big, but gentle."

I dipped my fingers into the grain and filled my palm.

"Keep your hand flat," don Pedro said.

I held out my palm.

The ox on the left nosed around my hand until every last grain was gone. The animal's fuzzy upper lip tickled me.

"That is Gallo," don Pedro said. "I think she likes you."

I reached up and scratched the bridge of her cream-colored face. Gallo's eyelids drooped in appreciation. I rubbed behind her floppy ears and the ox leaned into my hand, enjoying the attention. Jealous, Pinto nudged her over with his wide shoulders.

Don Pedro lifted the bucket and poured the grain into a long trough. The dreamy, ponderous beasts worked at snuffling up every speck.

"So señorita." Don Pedro leaned on the fence, putting

one foot on a lower rail. "What do you want to ask me?"

"Grace told me you sold your land at the same time as Luis."

"Ah." He pushed his hat back on his head. "The national park." He watched the oxen eat in silence.

"So, um — I was wondering if you could tell me, you know — if there was anything weird. About what happened." Jeez. How could I be a writer and yet be so bad with words? I would have been an awful private investigator. I couldn't even ask a decent question.

"Come with me," don Pedro said. He straightened and pushed away from the fence. "I will show you something."

He led me around to the other side of his house. A wooden shed stood smartly, looking as though it had just been built and was proud of its newness. We went inside and don Pedro pointed at one wall. "See this?" he asked.

"A wagon wheel?"

"An ox cart wheel," he said. "In this wheel is the story of Costa Rica."

I began to think I was never going to get a coherent answer from this man.

"You flew in to San José, no?"

"Yes," I said.

"San José is in the central valley. Here." He pointed at the center of the wheel.

"The ox cart wheel is Costa Rica?"

"A — how do you call it? A metaphor. The central valley was known as the Meseta, the plateau or tableland. The Spanish settlers, when they came, found the coasts too hot and horrible for their tastes. They like the nicer weather in the Meseta."

As the heat of the day began to weigh, I could appreciate their preference.

"You are from the States?" he asked.

"I am."

"Your country expanded one way. East to West." He swept his hand through the air, from right to left. "My country, it expanded out from the center." Using both hands, he created an ever widening circle.

"Like the spokes on the wheel," I said.

"You catch on," he said. "But the people of the Meseta had a problem."

"What kind of problem?"

Don Pedro rummaged around on a cluttered work bench. He picked up a fine-tipped paint brush and held it out to me. "You can help me," he said.

I took the brush. "What do you need help with?"

Don Pedro continued to search through the clutter on the table. "I will tell you," he said, "about the time my uncle was chased by a lithic sphere."

At that moment, I doubted this man would be able to focus on one topic long enough to answer my questions.

40

"So the spheres chase people?"

"I know what you think." Don Pedro gave me a wave of dismissal. "I would not believe it either, but my mama, she told me the story. And she never lied."

"Okay."

Don Pedro found another brush. "My mother and uncle were maybe ten and twelve years old," he said. "Their parents — my grandparents — took them to a fancy hotel. They played in the courtyard. Alone."

He found two small paint cans. He pulled them off a set of shelves that lined the wall. "A sphere the size of a soccer ball sat on a pedestal in the garden." He shook the cans and set them on the table.

"Well, that sphere, it jumped right off the pedestal and chased my uncle over the whole courtyard. No matter which way he ran, the sphere spun and rolled after him."

Don Pedro picked up a flathead screwdriver. "My mama and uncle escaped into the hotel and told their parents what happened." He pried open the cans of paint. "When they all went back out to the courtyard, the ball was back on the pedestal. As though it never moved."

He went outside and came back with a stick. He snapped it in half and stirred the paint. "My mama," he said, "she believed the spheres were not of this world."

Ah — aliens, I thought. I refrained from saying it out loud. Instead, I asked "So what do you think the spheres mean?"

He waved a hand towards the heavens. "The sun, the moon, the stars."

"That would explain the different sizes."

Don Pedro picked up the open cans of paint. "Some mysteries are not to be explained," he said. "Which color do you like?"

I peered into the cans. "Blue."

"I take the red then." He handed me the can, and together with the brush, I carried it outside. I followed him around to the back of the shed where a carport-like structure had been erected. Underneath was a wooden cart. It had one wheel.

"I am making this cart for Gallo and Pinto," don Pedro said. "You help me paint it."

I took in the cart with its intricate geometric designs. One section, around where the wheel would go, remained unpainted, a design painstakingly sketched onto the wood with a pencil. "Oh, I don't know if I can—"

"You must," he said. "Then it will always remember you."

Yeah — as the one who left an ugly blotch on its side.

"Por favor." Don Pedro pulled up two stools. "All who visit me paint. This is for the community."

Reluctantly, I squatted on the stool and balanced the can of paint on one knee.

"See here?" Don Pedro pointed to a beautiful design that curved around the front of the cart. A steady hand had made the lines clean, sharp. "The girl, Rosa, she paint that."

I set my brush on the top of my leg, reached out, and touched Rosa's design.

"You are searching for her, no?"

I met don Pedro's eyes. The old man possessed more clarity than he'd led me to believe. "Yes," I said. "I thought her disappearance might have something to do with the money from the land sale."

"The money?" Don Pedro wrinkled his brow as he brushed red paint onto the cart in a slow arc. "No, I do not think so."

He didn't say any more, so I dipped the tip of my brush into the can on my knee and dabbed it onto a teardrop-shaped design. As I worked, I became so engrossed that don

Pedro startled me when he spoke again.

"The people who lived in the Meseta, they had a problem."

"Oh right." I watched as don Pedro swept on some more red paint. "What was the problem?" I asked.

"Snow."

"Snow?" Just when I thought the man was lucid. "In the tropics?"

Don Pedro reached into the cart and pulled out a sealed jar. Several red berries — a little smaller than cherries — rolled around inside. "We call this Costa Rican snow." He held up the jar. "When the flowers of this plant bloom in the Meseta, they blanket the hills with white."

"What is it?"

"After the flowers, comes the fruit. Inside of the berries are beans."

"Coffee?"

"Sí."

"But why the problem? Wasn't coffee an important export?"

"The most important," he said. "The plant came from Africa. The Spanish brought it. Before that, Costa Rica was the poorest colony."

"Despite being named the Rich Coast."

"Sí. One day, a ship from Europe sailed into a harbor on the Pacific side. The captain, before he could go around the tip of South America, he need ballast for his ship."

"So he filled his holds with coffee beans."

"After that, Europeans could not get enough Meseta coffee. The flavor comes from the volcanic ash in the soil. Wonderful."

"So I still don't get it. What was the problem?"

"No way to ship the beans to the Atlantic coast. So the coffee had to travel over muddy, washed-out ox cart tracks all the way down to the Pacific coast."

"Amazing," I said. "They carried coffee all the way around the tip of South America."

"It was not until many years later that Costa Rica built a railroad to the Atlantic. The Jungle Train, they call it."

"Don Pedro, this is all very interesting, but what does it have to do with Rosa?"

"Ah." He plopped his brush into the paint can and set it aside. "The land down here is not so good for farming. My parents owned many hectares, but they could not even harvest the trees. The terrain was too rough."

"So it was still virgin forest," I said, "which is why the national park wanted it."

"I was happy to sell my parent's *finca* to the park," don Pedro said. "I bought Gallo and Pinto and the ox cart with some of the money. Together we will teach the children and the tourists our culture."

"But I still don't see what this has to do with Rosa."

"You remember the ox cart wheel?"

"On the wall."

"The middle of the wheel is the central valley. The spokes are routes of expansion — the ox cart tracks, the jungle train, the highway from San José. Some people think it is not enough."

"I don't get it."

"On the day Luis sold his land, a man showed up to protest against the sale. He did not want Luis to sell to the national park."

"Why not?"

"He wanted to push the spokes out more. To develop

the Golfo Dulce on the coast. Build hotels for tourists."

"Which he would not be able to do if the land became part of the national park."

"Sí. It was a paper park only. At least until the land was sold willingly."

"Who was this man?" I asked.

"I do not know his name. A foreigner, I think. He runs a rafting business."

"With a big truck?"

"Ah — you know him then?"

"I have seen him."

All of us had seen him.

All of us had heard Tarzan call him a bastard.

41

I examined the pan of crumbs — the remnants of the tres leches.

My watch said it was two o'clock. I had stayed to help don Pedro finish painting the ox cart. I had even helped him put the wheel back on. When I left, he was looking for the yoke. He wanted to take the ox cart and Gallo and Pinto out for a spin.

In the meantime, the canopy walkers had swooped back into the lodge and devoured all of the lunch. I stared with longing at the empty dessert pan. With the exception of a few crumbs, the vultures had picked it clean.

My stomach gnawed at my insides. I had to find some

food. The kitchen was closed, so I made a decision. I would hike to the village and get something to eat at the *pulperia*.

The brilliancy of this plan revealed itself as I trudged down the road. While I scrounged up some food, I could also question the shopkeeper. If anyone was up on the town gossip, it would definitely be her. I bet she could give me all kinds of dirt on the bastard outfitter.

I arrived at the *pulperia* and ordered a *refresco*.

The shopkeeper whipped it up and handed it to me.

I could not figure out a way to be sly, so I just came out with it. "Are you familiar with the outfitter that runs raft trips? We saw him the other day when we were on the river."

"Sí."

That was all she said. I was going to have to remember to ask open-ended questions. "So — do you know his name?"

"No."

Shoot, I did it again. "Can you tell me where to—" Wait. I needed a question she couldn't answer with a yes or no. I tried again. "Where can I find him?"

The shopkeeper shrugged and took the money for the drink.

Maybe I needed to be more specific. "Does he have an office somewhere? Here in town?"

"No."

I sipped my drink. I was so bad at this.

"That man," she said unexpectedly, "he is based in Golfito. His guests, they spend more time shuttling back and forth in those *feo* trucks than they do on the river."

That was better. "Golfito?" On these roads, that was at least two hours away. Maybe more.

"Why you need to find this man?" she asked.

"No particular reason. Just curious." I took my change. Then I hunkered down at an outdoor table and brooded.

It had taken my entire morning to dig up the information on the rival outfitter. I even helped a man paint an ox cart. And yet where did it get me?

Golfito was hours away. Even if I was able to convince Anthony to drive me there in his car — which he wouldn't do since he didn't want me involved — what could I do when I got there? I mean, it was one thing to casually wander into a place here in the village. It was another thing entirely to drive two hours and march into a man's business demanding answers.

I could pose as a customer. But then what? There was no way to sneakily weave questions into a conversation like: Did you kidnap a man's daughter to get back at him for selling his land? Did you hire a man called Tarzan to do it for you and then kill him because he knew your dirty secret?

Preposterous.

A girl and boy approached the table.

As often happens when I traveled, I had lost track of the days of the week. Apparently, this wasn't a school day.

"Hi," the girl said shyly. Both children eyed my untouched drink.

"Would you like one?" I asked.

They both nodded eagerly.

I took them to the shop and allowed them to each pick out a drink and a small pastry. They wanted candy, but I figured all mothers were the same, carefully controlling their children's sugar intake.

The owner of the shop handed me the fruity drinks. "You do not have to do this," she said. "Some of the children learn to use their big eyes to advantage with the tourists."

"That's okay," I said. "I'm happy to."

I had recognized the children as soon as I saw them. I had danced with the boy at the school. The girl had been his partner during the performance. I felt that buying them a treat was the least I could do.

The three of us sat at the table.

"So you don't have school today?" I asked, though the answer was obvious. I couldn't think of anything else to say.

They shook their heads and slurped at their straws.

"What do you kids do on your days off?" I asked.

The boy puffed up proudly. "I work with my brother and my father."

The girl rolled her eyes. "Do not listen to my brother. He thinks he is *muy importante*."

"Well, I'm sure he is. What do you do that's so important?" I asked the boy.

"My father, he guide horse trips for tourists into the park. Tomorrow he have a group. Today I help my brother round up the horses."

"That is a big job."

The boy polished off his pastry. His older sister sat primly eating hers. The boy jumped up from the table, shoved his hands in his pockets, and kicked at some rocks.

"And you?" I asked the girl. "What do you like to do?"

"I help my mother. Sometimes, she brings home bottles of shampoo and I put on the labels."

Click.

The sound came from the boy. The girl and I glanced over at him. He'd taken his hands out of his pockets. He held something in one of them.

Click, clack.

I couldn't see what he was holding. I assumed it was a toy

of some kind. I turned back to the girl. "And do you play, too? You and your brother?"

"The people at the lodge, they built a playground for us. Also we like to play marbles. And sometimes the lodge has a movie night."

Click, clack, snap.

The girl spun on her brother. "Stop it! You will bother the lady."

"No. No, it's all right. What do you have there?"

The boy held out his hand. He uncurled his fingers and revealed a small, pink barrette.

It looked familiar to me. My mind flashed around to various scenes, trying to place it. I pulled out my camera and whisked through the collection of images until I found the ones I had taken at the school.

I stopped at a photo of Rosa. She was in the classroom, her elbow on her desk, gazing up at the boy next to her. The wisps of her hair were held back with a pink barrette.

I spun on the boy. "Where did you get that?"

The boy's hand closed possessively around the barrette. "I found it on the ground. I did not steal it."

"I know," I said, realizing my tone had frightened him. "Can you please tell me where you found it?"

"With my brother this morning. Two of the horses were far from the rest. They wander over the border with the park. I find them eating by an old farmhouse there."

I leaped up in excitement, spilling my melted drink. "Will you tell me how to get there?"

The boy gave me directions as I tried to mop up the mess I had made. As soon as I was certain I understood, I rushed off, leaving the children to wonder if I was *loco en la cabeza*. Crazy in the head.

42

I rushed off without thinking, without making a plan.

I didn't tell anyone where I was going. Not my dad, not Anthony, not Stacy.

I knew the route. The boy's directions sent me down the path I had taken with Anthony just two days before. Had so little time passed?

I didn't stop until I reached the blue-black pool with the white ribbon fall. I went still and cocked my head, as if listening to an echo.

Why do you do this?

Anthony's words were still there, ping-ponging around the clearing like the light that skittered over the pool.

Why was I doing this?

I gave Anthony a reason, but it was a shallow one — my need to be a hero on an adventure. I knew that it was something more, but I was unable to reveal that part of myself to him, or even to me.

Why was I doing this?

Why was I charging off to find Rosa, all alone and ill-prepared? Was I trying to prove myself to Kaylee? Was it a desperate attempt to be independent of my father? Or was it nothing more than plain old vanity making me want to be the hero?

I touched the rocks where we had sat. The surface was rough and unpolished and I knew that the rocks were still young, still naïve. They had not been forced to change under intense pressure and heat. They had not been eroded down under the relentless passage of days. They were still what they had been the day they first bubbled forth and cooled in the humid air.

Perhaps the people who lived here before had felt a kinship with the stones, sensed an innate spirituality in them. Perhaps that is why they hauled stones for miles and fashioned them into spheres, a symbol of perfection.

I pressed my palms into the rock and gazed down at the pool. I remembered Anthony tossing a pebble into its depths. The small stone had broken through and changed the surface of the water, sending ripples in every direction.

I doubted it changed anything beneath.

I looked at the spot where I had sat and remembered Anthony sliding towards me, bridging the space between the two rocks.

It occurred to me that people must have always connected like this, coming together among the stones. From the first people that crawled under the shelter of rocks to sleep. From the first families that tugged stones together to make fire pits and teepee rings. From the first humans that piled up rocks to form altars and pyramids and walls and homes.

How many events in my life had centered around stones?

Like the time my dad and I sat on two rocks under the night sky, a campfire simmering in the desert, the sand emanating the day's heat, the mesquite bushes releasing their scent.

On that night, my dad told me that he was going to move out, that he and my mom were splitting up, like two stones rolling apart.

Four years later, under another night sky, with the stars somewhat altered in their apparent orbit, my dad told me another rock-shifting event. He was going to remarry.

Then there were the rocks on the overlook. The two that were just right for sitting, where Kaylee and I shared our life secrets. First crushes and first kisses and dreams of careers and dreams of love, revelations of failures and break-ups and the crossing of thresholds. Life secrets were so easy to share when we sat on those rocks.

Death secrets were not.

I stopped trying to see into the dark pool. I climbed on top of the rocks. I shut my eyes and relived Anthony's kiss, recalled the connection I felt when he looked at me. Some part of me knew it could not last, that in a few days I would leave and eventually the reality of his life would call him back, too. But despite what might come, the moment we'd shared on these rocks had felt like a genuine connection.

I splayed out my fingers and absorbed the rock beneath me. It was a symbol of strength. A strength I needed now if I was to bring Rosa home.

I opened my eyes and took one last look at the ribbon fall.

I stepped away from the pool.

I stepped away from the rocks.

I stepped into unknown territory.

It's strange how the importance of a moment in time can alter the fabric of space.

No longer does the world spin around with you riding along as a passive traveler. The paths of the planets warp and change until the rotation of an entire galaxy centers on you. The universe now seems to be either intently watching you or steadfastly turning away. Each step propels the vortex forward and the continuum rests in your every footfall.

You have transformed from a meaningless floating scrap of space debris into a celestial body, destined to streak across the sky in a sweeping blaze or peter out into nothingness at the far reaches of the solar system.

This must have been something of what Kaylee felt on that night half a year ago.

"Through the door," she said. "Someone pushed me."

Five months in Cambodia working a story on the sex trade. Five months creeping along in the shadows of a woman, a survivor who returned to the red-light districts and brothels of her childhood to save other girls.

Kaylee immersed herself in that horrific world, becoming obsessed with one girl, a child snatched when her mother turned her back. It happened in a busy city, at a busy fair, on a busy day — the girl's seventh birthday.

"The day she was taken," Kaylee said. "The day she was sold. The survivors have a name for that. They call it *The day my god died.*" She and the other rescuers tracked the girl down, only to find she'd been sold again.

"We finally found the right place," Kaylee said. "We got there and I was afraid to go inside." I recalled the way Kaylee rubbed her hands together when she told me this. If she had been holding a stick, it would have burst into flames.

"Through the door," she said. "Someone pushed me."

The crack of a twig snapped me back.

I peered down the path that stretched behind me. I could not see anything. Here beneath the canopy, it was like twilight in the middle of the day. A wave of fear made me wish my dad was with me.

I pushed forward again. I was not going to allow myself to think like that. Hadn't I wanted my dad to notice the woman I had become? This was something I had to do on my own.

Besides, if my dad knew where I was right then, he'd deploy an entire battalion to come and get me. He would not understand.

No — that wasn't true.

My dad might have been a veteran of war, but that didn't change the fact that he was a Chihuahua-herding goofball under it all.

He would understand.

He would know what it meant to save a life. In Vietnam he'd saved lots of lives. Other boys like himself. Boys that had gone on to have families, daughters like me.

Like Kaylee.

She, too, had saved lives. The lives of daughters. Girls sold or bartered away like so many old cars cluttering the driveway and costing more in repairs than they were worth to maintain.

My best friend immersed herself in that world, exposing it, splashing it on the pages of a magazine, drawing a tide of sympathy and money to a problem that would not go away.

My father and my friend. They had seen and experienced and done things. Their lives meant something in this world. They had come away profoundly changed, understanding things I never could. They knew of the deepest hells of human existence and had tried to make a difference, had tried to make sense of it all.

My father had succeeded. He dove into the remainder of his life with a reckless fervor that annoyed but also inspired.

My friend tripped, sliding into a dark place where I should have seen her wallowing. I should have reached out a hand and pulled her back into the light. But in my own self-centered meanderings, I passed her by.

Now she represented my greatest fear. A fear of stumbling through life, oblivious and useless, making not the slightest ripple in the sea or adding the tiniest thread to the tapestry.

Living a life that did not somehow impact.

I was afraid of being like the old cars, useless and costing more for the world to maintain then the service I gave in return.

This was why I was doing this.

This was why I had to save Rosa.

This was why the person who took her had to pay.

43

The jungle darkened.

The canopy thickened. Plants crowded around me like a gang of loping monsters.

I hoped more than anything that I would find Rosa soon. I hoped more than anything that I would find Rosa safe.

A scream pierced the air.

My heart skittered around in my chest before my brain explained that the sound was only the creepy call of a howler monkey.

Time stretched and contracted like a rubber band.

An archway of light glowed ahead.

I emerged into a meadow. The sun sizzled on the thick, low-cut grass. This must have been where the boy's family pastured the horses. A pile of horse manure on the path confirmed this.

It wouldn't be long now.

I crossed the open area, feeling strangely exposed.

On the other side, I melted back into the shadow of the trees. A brook squabbled ahead. I moved closer to the sound and then, before I could anticipate it, I was at the house.

The wooden structure hunkered over the stream, as though depressed that its owners had abandoned it.

Could this be where Rosa was hidden?

I waded across the creek — stepping on rocks in the deeper parts — and halted before the front door.

I placed a foot on the bottom step and tested it to make sure it would hold my weight. I stepped over the next one, which was broken on one end, and planted both feet on the porch.

I studied the doorknob. I cocked my head and listened. Nothing.

No calling for help. No plaintive crying. Nothing.

I reached up. My hand trembled. I closed my fingers around the knob and turned. I expected it to be locked, but it gave easily and the door swung inward.

Darkness spilled out. I stepped across the threshold and then stopped, allowing my eyes to adjust. A grimy smudge of light filtered in through a small window. Dust motes hung in the light, as though waiting for something to happen.

I moved forward until I was in the center of the house's main room. I spun in a slow circle, my eyes searching out every dark shape: a lopsided table, a broken chair, a collapsed bed, a basin, shards of old pots. A cobweb fluttered. I jumped at the movement.

Then I heard the breathing.

I wheeled towards the sound. The soft rise and fall of air came from the darkness pooling in a far corner, out of reach of the weak light that filtered in through the window and followed me through the door.

"Who's there?" I directed my wobbly question at the shadow.

My words disturbed the specks of dust. They quivered, as though they were anxious to answer my question, but did not know how.

"Aurora," the pool of darkness said. "It's me."

44

The room was close and hot, yet for some reason, I shivered.

The dust motes grew more agitated. The scent of mildew thrust up my nose. The entire slumping building smelled of neglect.

Standing in the light made me feel vulnerable. Darkness gave the advantage. I moved toward the inky pool.

I had come all this way seeking answers. All this way to find what I had been looking for.

Now it was right here, hiding in that black corner.

And I had no idea what to make of it.

"Grace."

The lodge manager stepped into the swath of light. Even in the murkiness, her black hair shimmered.

"What're you doing here?" I asked.

"The same thing you are."

"Is she here?"

"No," Grace said.

My hopes slumped like the house. "How did you know?"

Grace inclined her head. "I have known for a while."

"You have?" I said. "I don't understand. Why didn't you say something?"

"I was afraid."

"Because of Tarzan?"

"Tarzan?" she repeated.

"The raft guide."

"He is the reason I came here," she said.

"I don't understand. Do you mean you talked to him before he died?"

"No," she said. "I was afraid to be blamed."

"Blamed? For what?"

"His death."

"What? Why would you—"

"Tell me who you are." Grace stood so still, with the light from the window illuminating her, that the floating specks of dust around her also grew still. Now they remained suspended in the glowing air, vibrating with expectation.

"Who are you?" she asked again.

"I'm—"

"A writer. I know. But really — you are something like a detective."

"A what?" I said, stunned. "Why in the world would you think that?"

"You have been questioning me," Grace said. "Watching me. Following me."

Something wasn't right here. Watching? Following?

What was she talking about?

I reached into my pocket and pulled out the pink barrette. I held it out for Grace to see. "A boy in the village found this," I said. "He found it near this house."

Grace considered the bit of plastic in my hand. "I brought Rosa here," she said, "after you found the body. But she would not stay. This place — it frightened her."

I was silent.

Grace looked at me with steady eyes. "I know what I did was wrong."

"Now, wait a minute," I said. "Let me get this straight." I had trouble believing what I was about the say. "You took Rosa? You're the kidnapper?"

Now Grace was silent.

"And the ransom note?" I continued. "That was you?"

"You knew this," she said.

"Will you stop saying that? I didn't know anything."

Grace opened her mouth as if to speak, then closed it.

"Run this by me one more time," I said. "You're Rosa's kidnapper? But why? You're so — so nice."

A tear speared down Grace's cheek.

"Oh — don't do that," I said. "I have no idea what you thought, but I haven't been following you. Or watching you. I thought Tarzan took Rosa. And when he showed up dead, I didn't know what to think."

"I gave myself away then."

"I — well, yes. But maybe if you bring her back, it won't be so bad. I'm sure there's an explanation." I had not expected that I would react this way when I found the person who took Rosa. I certainly had not expected that I would try to give her a way out.

What was I doing?

Grace looked at her feet.

"Isn't there?" I asked. "An explanation?"

"Rosa is mine."

"What?"

"Mine. My child. My baby."

I gaped at her. "How can that be?" I did some fast calculations. Grace couldn't have been more than twenty-four. Twenty-five tops.

"I gave birth to her when I was sixteen."

Rosa was about nine. "So — Luis adopted her?"

"No," Grace said. "She was taken from me."

"But — why? Why would someone do that?"

"People who have little," Grace said. "They look for a way out. I have two older sisters that went off with men, hoping for a better life. They were young. Fifteen, sixteen. The oldest, she did well. The other—" Grace moved out of the light. "When I was fifteen, I met a German tourist. I thought we were in love. I thought he would take me away, too."

I regarded Grace in the dimness of the old house. Now that she had stepped out of the light, her black hair lost its shimmer and shadows pooled under her eyes. The truth of what had happened started to make sense. Here was a story that played out in most any culture.

"He left you pregnant."

Grace nodded. "My parents are very traditional," she said. "They were ashamed of me and sent me away to stay with my oldest sister. But when the time came, there was no money for a doctor and they brought me back here. My uncle came from Golfito. He works at the clinic there. He delivered the baby and told my parents he had found someone to adopt."

"Luis?"

"No, I do not know who," Grace said. "Luis's wife — many times she miscarried babies. She was pregnant at the same time I was. She carried her baby almost the whole way, but it came early, while Luis was away, and the baby died."

"Your uncle swapped the babies?" I said. "That's unbelievable."

"Luis's wife suffered from losing a lot of blood. I do not know if she knew. Nobody else did. Not Luis. Not me."

I found myself wanting to reach out to Grace, to connect with her, to comfort her. "How did you find out?"

"A year ago, a doctor diagnosed me with ovarian cancer. When I told you I stayed with my sister a few months ago, it was to have a hysterectomy."

"So now you can't have children. Grace — I'm sorry."

"I cannot have more children. You understand — I had to know what became of my baby. I begged my sister to tell me what she knew. When she did, I was shocked. My child, my daughter, she was right here."

"But why ask for the money? Why not just take her?"

"Do you not think Luis owed me at least that? Besides, I did not ask for all his money. Only some. I needed it so I could afford to go away."

"You never intended to give Rosa back."

"Why would I? Working here at the lodge, I had to see her everyday. Do you have any idea what that was like for me?"

I had no answer.

"All I want is to be a mama to my little girl," Grace said. "Luis has his own child now."

I remembered how I felt when I held Luis's baby boy— the mix of longing and fear at the thought of having a child of my own. Being a mother was still a possibility for me —

an open door. A door that had unfairly slammed shut on Grace. "I don't see why you thought I knew."

"You watched me," she said, "in the lodge while I was working. You were looking at the phone after I called my sister. You were there when I tried to take the money."

The absurdity of the situation struck me. If only Grace had known the truth. That I watched her because I envied her hair. That I looked at the phone because of Tarzan. That I felt guilty for scaring the kidnapper away from the money. I replayed the scenes as she saw them, watching them from her point of view. It was like using a different filter.

But I still didn't understand one thing. "Where has Rosa been all this time?"

Somewhere outside, a man's voice shouted my name.

Grace moved back into the dusty pool of light. I sensed she was preparing to bolt.

I put my hand on her arm. "Tell me where she is, Grace."

She tried to pull away from me.

I clamped down tighter. "Where is Rosa?"

Grace did not respond.

"You have to give her back."

The man called out again. He was closer now. I recognized the voice as belonging to my father. Somehow he'd found me. Somehow he'd managed to interfere again.

I pulled sharply on Grace's arm. "Do you want to be blamed for Tarzan's death?"

Fear flicked over her face.

My next words came out slow and insistent. "Tell—me—where—she—is."

My dad's foot scraped across the front steps.

Grace's eyes pleaded.

Her desperation filled me with fury. The woman had caused so much suffering for Luis, for his family, for the villagers, for Rosa. She had to pay for what she'd done. I only needed to hold on to her, to wait for my dad to come in. Then we could take her away. Then we could turn her in. Then we could find Rosa.

But when I looked at her again, it wasn't Grace's eyes staring at me with all that emptiness and loss. It was Kaylee's.

Go away, Kaylee.

"Please, Aurora."

Now is not the time.

"Please forgive me for what I did. It was a terrible, terrible mistake."

I was never really sure who spoke the words. All I knew was that my hand had let go of Grace's arm. Facing each other, we listened as my dad approached the front door. His feet weighed heavily on the porch. The rotting boards groaned under his every footfall.

Grace relented. "Rosa is in my cabin," she said in a rush of hushed words. "She has been there the whole time." She turned and fled out the back door.

I did not try to stop her.

45

We brought her home.

Yes Kaylee. We did.

My dad and I walked down the main street that led through the center of the village. Rosa walked between us.

Grace had told the truth. Rosa was in her room. No one suspected the lodge manager, so no one thought to look in her cabin.

There we found Rosa, idly flipping through a book, completely unaware of any danger. She had looked up at me and my dad, her big brown eyes filled with curiosity, but not a hint of fear. Shyly, she told us that Grace had intercepted her on the way home from school, that Grace had said her brother had the flu and her parents went to the city to see a doctor. Rosa told us that she was supposed to stay with Grace until her family got back. She wasn't to leave the room in case she also came down with the flu.

Rosa was a good girl. She obeyed.

How easy it would have been for Grace to take the girl away. All she would have needed to do is say they were going to the city to visit Rosa's parents and her brother.

Thank goodness Grace hadn't taken the money.

News of Rosa's return must have riffled through the entire village. People lined the street along either side.

As we watched, Luis emerged from his house.

Rosa picked up her feet and skipped over to him. My dad and I had not contradicted Grace's story, so as far as Rosa knew, she was the one welcoming her father home.

Luis dropped to his knees and gathered Rosa into his arms. "My niña." He brushed back her hair and kissed her cheek.

Rosa threw her arms around his neck and kissed him back.

The people lining the street cheered.

I stood at a respectful distance, my own father next to me. He started to speak and his voice startled me. It wasn't so much the suddenness, but the tone. It sounded so — gentle.

Very uncharacteristic.

"When you were a little girl," he said. "Sometimes — when I couldn't sleep at night, I'd get a pillow and blanket and go into your room and lie on the floor."

I couldn't believe what he was saying.

"For some reason," he continued, "listening to you breathe would make everything better. I'd fall asleep, right there, on your floor, and your mother would find me in the morning."

I couldn't take my eyes off Luis and Rosa.

"I simply cannot imagine," my dad said, "what that poor man just went through."

I couldn't say a word.

46

*O*n the inside, I waged an emotional war.

On the outside, I was just another guest at the Piedras Blancas Lodge waiting for dinner to be served.

The meal was going to be late. Apparently, the cooks had abandoned their posts that afternoon to welcome Rosa home.

After I told Luis and the police the truth about what happened to Rosa, a few people went on the hunt, trying to find Grace. Somewhere deep down, I hoped they wouldn't catch her.

What the heck was wrong with me?

I should have been all warm and glowy feeling after watching Rosa's reunion with her father. I should have felt that I had come to an understanding with Kaylee. I should have wanted to hug my dad.

But I didn't feel any of these things.

Instead of feeling happy about my part in bringing Rosa home, I felt shame. Rosa was never truly in danger. She wasn't one of the poster children in the airport, she wasn't the girl Kaylee searched for, she wasn't in the clutches of a murderer. Her kidnapper wasn't even a villain, just a sad woman who wanted to be a mother.

Maybe my involvement in Rosa's disappearance had been nothing more than a selfish desire. I had wanted to be the hero, so I imagined Rosa's life was at stake. My ambition had run away with me. Had I really wished that she was in danger just so I could save her?

As for Kaylee, I could understand why she did what she did. I maybe even could forgive her. But would I ever forget?

And speaking of forgiveness, why couldn't I bring myself to make up with my dad? He waved a white flag and I ignored it. I knew in my heart he was telling me how much he loved me, but in my head I couldn't get past the fact that he thought of me as a little girl. A little girl asleep in my bed. A little girl like Rosa. Was he ever going to stop thinking of me as a girl and notice the woman I had become?

A trilling noise sounded in a dark corner of the lodge.

My dad sat in front of an old computer. From the scowl on his face, I figured he was trying to use a dial-up internet connection.

Today he wore a T-shirt that Nelle ordered from one of those photo websites. The entire front of the neon blue shirt was taken up by the giganticly enlarged head of my dad's favorite Chihuahua. The name of the dog was Calico, but for some inexplicable reason, my dad called her Bozo Bear.

The annoying yapper was in charge of my dad's household. Since she was only three millimeters tall, she bossed everyone — human and canine alike — from her throne of power, my dad's lap.

I suppose even rat-dogs have alphas.

I wondered how Bozo was faring with my dad gone. I also wondered if I was ever going to speak to my dad again.

Anthony sidled up next to me. He must have sensed the weird vibe. "You want to get out of here?" he asked.

"Sure," I said. "Why not?"

The computer modem squealed as Anthony and I left the lodge.

"You and your dad still not talking?"

"No."

"Sorry if it's because of me."

"Don't flatter yourself. You were just the catalyst."

Anthony strolled down one of the paths that wound through the grounds. I followed.

"I take it there's been some friction?" Anthony asked.

"I was mad about him coming here."

"How's that work, anyway?"

"How's what work?"

"You and your dad working together."

"It doesn't."

"You sure about that?"

"We've written one article together. About a trip we took to Vietnam. I guess people liked it."

"You co-authored it?"

"We wrote separately, thank heaven for that."

"So it's like a he-said, she-said kind of thing?"

"I suppose. Travel articles are typically written by one person. That means readers only get one point of view."

"So you thought you'd try something different?" Anthony asked.

"No, my editor did," I said. "You see — typically, people don't travel alone. They go with a spouse, friend, whatever. So my editor thought readers would like more than one perspective."

"Sounds like a good idea to me."

"You don't have to work with my dad."

"True."

"He and I aren't supposed to compare notes or anything. We each write what we thought of a trip. Then our editor puts it together."

"I imagine you and your dad have a different take on things."

"Like night and day."

"Sometimes you need to see the dark in the light. And the light in the dark."

"Kaylee's words," I said. "When she gave me the filter."

"Maybe that's what she meant," Anthony said. "That the world's not black-and-white. That there's always more than one point of view."

"It ticks me off."

"Sorry, I shouldn't have brought it up."

"Not that."

"Working with your dad, then?"

"No. Yes. That, too. I mean what happened with Kaylee."

"With Kaylee?"

"I know, I'm a terrible person for saying that."

"Is that what all this was about?" he asked.

"All what?"

"You, going off to find Rosa without me, without your dad."

"Where is this coming from?"

"It was stupid of you to go off alone like that."

"Grace was hardly dangerous," I said.

"You didn't know who you were going to find out there. You could have been killed. Like Tarzan."

"You said that was an accident."

Anthony picked up his pace.

"What? What is it?"

"They found his kayak outside his room."

"So he wasn't on the water," I said.

"The police are now saying the bruise on his head had

markings that resemble—"

"A paddle."

"So there you go," Anthony said. "You suspected murder and yet you charged off alone, without telling anyone where you were going."

"What is your problem? Let it go."

"Did it ever occur to you there are people who care what happens to you?"

I crossed my arms. "Why'd you change the subject? I thought we were talking about Kaylee."

"You're not to blame, you know."

"Why couldn't she just tell me?" I said. "I needed the direct approach. I'm not good at picking up on subtle hints and mysterious clues."

"I've noticed."

"I don't need you—"

Anthony came to an abrupt halt. I bumped into him.

We stood on a secluded part of the path. Before us, a ray of sun seared the ground. Around us, the jungle chirruped loudly — the sound a mix of wind and trees and buzzing life.

Anthony put his hands on my waist and steered me into a dark shadow. "How do you know?"

"How do I know what?" I said.

"That you don't need me?"

"I—"

He pushed me against the rough bark of a tree. Pressed his body into mine. Sought my mouth. Kissed me hard.

Quick fear licked down my body. A slow longing trickled back up. "What the hell was that?"

"The direct approach."

"I didn't say you could do that."

"You didn't say I couldn't."

"I don't know anything about you."

"Sure you do." Anthony continued to press into me, his face close to mine.

My skin prickled at his nearness.

"You know that I'm a single archaeology professor from California who's got it bad for a certain sexy adventure traveler."

"I don't know that."

"You do now." He kissed along my neck. My blood pulsed hotly in my veins. My sleeve slid over my shoulder.

I inhaled sharply and pushed Anthony away. "I want to know more," I said.

"So do I." He moved in again.

"No," I said. "About archaeology."

Anthony gave me a playful smile. "And then what?"

"We'll see."

47

I decided it would be safer to continue our conversation at the lodge.

The setting would be more public.

The cooks offered a dish called *olla de carne*, a stew packed with beef, potatoes, carrots, plantains, yucca, and a pear-like vegetable called *chayote*. Anthony and I spooned up hearty bowlfuls of the stew. We paired it with rice and a dessert of *tamal asado*, a sweet cornmeal cake.

We chose a quiet corner away from the rest of the group. I caught Stacy's eye and she gave me an enthusiastic thumb's up. My dad frowned.

"Okay, shoot," Anthony said once we were settled. "And make your questions count."

"Why? What are you? A genie or something? I only get three questions?"

"You get as many as you like, but you're going to owe me for each one."

"Owe you what?"

"That's to be determined."

"I can't agree to a deal like that," I said.

"No questions. No answers."

"No 'And then what' either."

Anthony reconsidered. "I'll allow you to have executive veto power. But you're still going to owe me."

I didn't like the idea of owing Anthony anything, yet it gave me a curious thrill. "Fine," I said. "Veto power."

"I'll be keeping count," he said.

"Okay, here goes. I already know archaeology is the study of the human past. What I want to know is, what's bad about it?"

"What's bad about it?"

"You heard me."

"That's a weird question," he said.

"If I have to owe you, then you have to work for it."

"Is this the whole 'dark in the light' thing?"

"It's a challenge."

"Fine, I accept." He dunked his corn cake in the stew and thought for a moment. "In fact, I'll give you two."

"Don't be tricky. I'll still just owe you one."

"But it'll be a good one."

"As long as it doesn't get vetoed."

"Understood." Anthony winked at me. "Here's the first one — it's all made up."

"If you're going to mock me, there's no deal."

"I'm being dead serious. No pun intended."

"Ha, ha." I spooned up a bite of stew.

"Archaeologists are like any other researchers. They set out to investigate a problem. But since they're working with evidence that's incomplete, much of it becomes speculation. Archaeological data can provide valuable insight into the past. It can even form the basis of theories that explain human behavior. But in the end, it's all made up."

"So that's why there's always debate."

"Experts never agree," he said. "They all want to be right. It's like the old joke about future archaeologists thinking that televisions are religious altars."

"I'd hate to see what they'd think of toilets."

"We've all worshiped a toilet a time or two."

"Speak for yourself," I said. "What's the second thing?"

"That's easy."

"Okay — am I supposed to read your mind?"

"Digging is destructive."

"Destructive?"

"Sure. To learn about the past, we have to destroy it. As soon as an artifact is taken out of the ground, all context is lost. That's why we have to collect a lot of photos, field notes, drawings, soil samples, and so forth. This archive of data takes the place of the actual site. The real thing is gone forever."

"So why do it then if it's so destructive? Can't you just take a sample?"

"Sometimes. But a lot of digs are salvage operations.

Only archaeologists destroy in a scientific way. Digging up a site may be the only way to keep the information they contain from being wiped out by treasure hunters or land developers."

"Land developers."

"What?"

"Nothing. Just something about an ox cart wheel and spokes and— Never mind. It would take too long to explain."

"You owe me big time," he said. "You got a lot of information out of one question."

"I still have veto rights."

"I'll think of something you can't resist."

"Not likely."

"Touché," he said. "Now come on, what's your next hard-hitting question?"

"I'm not a reporter. But now that you mention it, I should at least pretend I'm getting some work done. Tell me what's been made up about this place."

Anthony sopped the last of his stew up with his *tamal asado*.

"I think that was supposed to be dessert," I said.

"I thought it was corn bread." He brushed the crumbs from his hands. "Besides — I had something else in mind for dessert."

Yikes. I opened myself up for that one.

"The Diquis."

"The Di— who?"

"Diquis. The people who used to live in this place."

"Oh, right."

Anthony told me the Diquis were the same people who made the gold jewelry that drove the Spanish invaders into a

211

greedy frenzy. He told me they were the same people whose ancestors left the mysterious stone spheres.

As he talked, I imagined the ancient ones moving through the rainforest, dancing circles around their fires, hunting and cooking, making love and war, cradling their babies, and laying their elders to rest.

Then they vanished.

"So here it is—" I said. "The real reason why you took a leave of absence."

"What can I say? I love my work." Anthony reached across the table and placed a hand over mine. "Love to play, too. It's time to pay up."

"What, already?" I drew my hand away.

"You owe me a kiss good night."

"Right here? In front of everybody?"

"Veto?"

"Damn right."

"Okay then, outside."

As soon as we were out of the lodge and hidden from view, Anthony pulled me to him. His kiss was tender, yet full of heat. Too soon, he pulled back and sauntered away.

I stayed in the same spot, feeling kind of melty inside.

Ugh — I had become the vapid heroine after all.

48

*P*hotographers can't see a thing.

What they see is light. Not objects or items or things. Light.

Light is what our eyes see. Light streams in through our pupils — which function like the aperture in a camera lens — and fires up the rods and cones at the back of our eyes. It's our brains that take this spectacular light show and assemble it into a picture of a thing.

At some point, all good photographers realize this.

They stop looking for things. They start looking for light.

Photographers see the way light washes over from the side, feathers in from behind, or filters down from above. They wait for a rock to glow red in the setting sun instead of allowing it to bleach dull in the glare of midday.

To a photographer, light caresses and brushes and polishes and burnishes. Light is everywhere.

And photographers can't see a thing.

The flower swayed in the breeze. I cursed it. Taking a macro shot of a delicate bloom is impossible if the plant won't stay still.

I had ventured into the gardens to shoot pictures of the exotic flowers. They bobbed all around me. Their vivid colors made them look edible.

This flower burned with the color of red hot candies. That flower's petals glistened like slivers of fresh coconut.

The flowers over there piled up color like big bowlfuls of oranges, apples, and bananas.

Every one of the flowers glistened with fat raindrops, reminding me of the dewy bottles that marketers plaster on the front of soda machines.

My imagination was running amok again.

It must have been all that talk the night before about digging up the past. Anthony's revelation about Tarzan's kayak being found by his room — not smashed to bits on a rock — had me wondering what really happened to the river guide.

At breakfast, I had heard whispered rumors that Grace killed him. I knew that was nonsense.

But there were a lot of unanswered questions. Like, who was Tarzan talking to that night on the phone? And why did he call the other outfitter a bastard? Not to mention — what was Tarzan doing up a stream with a paddle but no kayak? Did any of this relate to his death? Or was it really just an accident?

The flower stopped swaying. I tried to focus my camera.

Focus on the light. Not the thing.

The problem with focusing on the light was that the shadows got darker. Anyone who has tried to photograph people in front of a bright background knows this. To avoid underexposing the shot, a flash or a reflector must be used to lighten the shadows.

I suppose that is what's meant by shedding light on a subject.

When it came to the subject of Tarzan's death, it was the light I needed to see. The light that held the answers. But at the moment, I was entirely in the dark.

The flower was now perfectly still. I tried to focus my camera.

Focus on the—

Wait a minute. It's the camera that focuses, the camera that assembles the light into a picture.

Quickly, I gathered up my gear and packed it away. I had an idea.

I found him at the lodge.

Video-camera-kid. His head was buried in his laptop computer.

I plopped down in the chair across from him.

The kid did not look up.

"Excuse me," I said. "May I interrupt you for a minute?"

He held up his index finger.

I waited.

"Yeah, what is it?" He extracted his head from the computer.

"I was wondering if you could help me shed some light on a subject."

"How am I supposed to do that?"

"With your camera. You've been shooting video all week. I was hoping maybe I could look through some of it."

"Do you know my name?"

"Uh—" Video-camera-kid?

He thrust out his right hand.

I gave it a tentative shake.

"We should know each other's names if we're gonna work together. Yours is Aurora, like the northern lights."

"Right." I was embarrassed he knew my name and I didn't know his.

"Steve."

"Nice to meet you, Steve. Formally, I mean."

He grinned. "I'm just joking with you. I only know your name cause of Stacy. She's always like, Aurora this, and Aurora that. She's been in awe of you ever since she found out about your job."

"I'm sure she changed her mind after the rafting trip."

"I doubt it," Steve said. "I'm sorry, by the way, about the video with the—" He waved a hand through the air.

"The legs. No you're not."

"I'm not?"

"Sorry."

Steve retreated back into his computer. "So how can I help you?"

"I'm interested in shots with Tarzan in them," I said. Everyone in our tour group referred to the raft guide by the nickname Stacy gave him. "But you can skip the rafting. I've seen enough of that. I want shots of Tarzan in the lodge, at meals, at night, whenever."

"Sure, okay. Mind if I ask what you're looking for?"

"Hard to say. Maybe Tarzan talking with someone else or on the phone or doing something unusual."

Steve spun the laptop towards me. "Can do. Only thing is, I haven't edited any of this yet, so it's still just one big file. We'll have to jump around a bit. Where do you want to start?"

"Tarzan died some time after the raft trip. Did you see him again after that day? Like maybe that night when you all were drinking at the lodge?"

Steve thought for a moment. "No, I don't think I did."

"Okay then. Anything from the time we got here right up to the night before we went rafting."

Steve clicked on an icon and the screen sprang to life. A multi-media program opened and the video automatically started to play. The image was jerky, but I could tell that Steve had started filming on the plane ride to Costa Rica. The other two guys were making lewd gestures at the camera.

"Why don't we jump ahead?" Steve said.

He glided his finger over the touchpad. The cursor moved across a slider bar. Steve clicked. The image froze, then flashed to a new scene. This one was worse.

"Oops," Steve said. He reached for the touchpad.

"No, don't."

What I was viewing was all too familiar.

On the screen, the shot panned from the row of bungalows across the grounds to Tico's pond. I saw myself marching down the path.

I watched the screen in disbelief as I leaped sideways, hung my foot on a vine, tipped over backwards, tumbled off the path, and landed with my legs in the air.

"You were spying on me," I said.

"No, now wait a minute. That was our first morning here. I was trying to get a nice panorama shot. You just happened to be there."

"Right. Do you have anything on this video that's not humiliating to me?"

We spent the next hour scrolling through endless video of the previous seven days. Steve had clearly not learned the art of being selective.

At the end of the hour, we still had nothing.

I scooted back in my chair and let out a frustrated huff. "That was pointless."

"Maybe not. We spent the whole time focusing on what

was happening in the foreground. I jotted down time stamps for certain scenes. Places where there was a lot going on."

"Okay." I leaned forward again. "But I'm not sure it'll do any good."

"That's the spirit."

Thanks to Steve's foresight, this pass went much quicker. But we still didn't find anything.

"So much for that idea," I said.

"Don't give up yet. We've still got one more segment."

Steve had been working backwards through the video. Now he clicked near the beginning of the slider bar. A new scene popped up. Our first night at the lodge. I saw myself sitting next to Rosa. We were weaving palm leaf grasshoppers.

The image tilted and jumped around then went still. Steve must have set the camera down on a table while it was taping. His digital face filled the screen, then retreated.

I tried to concentrate on what was happening in the background. The lodge was dimly lit. It was difficult to make out anything. I gave up. "Steve, I'm sorry I took up so much of your time. I shouldn't have—"

"There he is."

"Where? I don't see anything."

"There. On the left edge of the screen. I think I saw him for just a second."

We continued to watch. Then I glimpsed Tarzan's long hair as it swished into the scene.

"See that?" Steve said. "I think he sat down at a table."

I peered closer at the dark image. "Is there someone with him? Can you tell?"

"Yeah, I think you might be right. Let me zoom in a little." Steve clicked on a few buttons and the image of Tarzan jumped forward. "There's definitely somebody there, but it's too dark. I can't make out who it is."

"Wait," I said. "What're they doing?"

"They're looking at something. A piece of paper, I think."

"It's big," I said. "When he picked it up, it looked like it had creases. As if it had been folded."

"Like a brochure."

"No—" I said, leaning back in my chair. "Like a map."

49

I was about to be guilty of breaking and entering.

Steve and I had watched the video three more times. He managed to improve the image each time by zooming in a little more, adjusting the contrast, or slowing down the speed. I was now certain that what we had seen was a map.

And I wanted to find it.

Now I was outside Tarzan's room pretending I could stare a hole through the door with my super-heroine vision.

Unlike the guest lodging, the staff quarters were not cute little adjoining bungalows. Instead — with the exception of the manager's cabin — the staff quarters were more like permanent tents.

Shaped like a child's drawing of a house, Tarzan's tent was square with a triangle roof. Made of heavy canvas draped over a metal frame, the tent perched on top of a raised platform. This platform extended out from under the tent to make a porch.

On the porch sat a red kayak.

I ascended the four steps that led up to the porch. I was surprised to see that the entrance to Tarzan's room was not a flimsy canvas tent flap, but a real door attached to the metal frame.

I reached for the knob and then I hesitated.

I had never done anything like this before. I had never broken into a place and entered without permission. A small part of me hoped the door would be locked. Then I would be off the hook.

I rotated the knob.

The door swung open. I found myself peering into a dark rectangle. It wasn't too late. I hadn't crossed the threshold yet. I could still turn back.

I placed one foot through the door. Then the other foot.

There. It was done. I was officially a trespasser.

The room was a mess. I couldn't tell if Tarzan had been a slob or if the police had tossed his stuff. I prowled through, careful not to touch a thing.

The river guide had owned every imaginable piece of rafting gear. Heaped in the corners of the room were paddles and oars, ropes and D-rings, neoprene booties and gloves, wetsuits and paddling jackets, dry bags and life vests, helmets, river sandals, a box for an inflatable kayak, an electric pump, a foot pump, and a bunch of other stuff I couldn't identify.

I did not see a map.

I paused by Tarzan's bed. Two books lay on his nightstand. *Desert Solitaire* and *On the River* by Edward Abbey.

I suddenly felt sorry for Tarzan. He'd been pompous and a little ridiculous, but underneath it all he was a lover of rivers. The man had a heart. And he'd been way too young to die.

Tarzan's tent did not have windows. Instead, it had close-knit netting that allowed the air in and kept the bugs out. Patterns of shadow and light fluttered across the fabric. The filtered light bathed everything in the room with a greenish tint.

I circled again, but I still did not see anything that resembled a map. I wanted to avoid disturbing Tarzan's things, but I was foolish to think the map would be in plain sight. I tried to figure out a likely hiding place.

Someone approached the tent. Soft footfalls padded across the leafy ground. A shadow passed along the far wall. I hoped it would move on by.

Instead, the shadow thudded up the steps.

I figured it was just my father butting in again, but I didn't want to risk waiting around to find out. If it was the police, I would be in a lot of trouble. I searched for a way to escape.

A bathroom was attached to the back of the tent. I didn't know if it had a way out, but it was my only option. I darted over to the bathroom and scooted inside just as the knob on the front door started to spin.

The bathroom walls were not made of canvas. They were made of solid wood. The only opening was a small window above the toilet.

Behind me, in the main room, the front door swished open.

I dashed across the bathroom and hopped up on the lid of the toilet. I cranked the handle on the window and opened it as far as it would go. I hoped I wasn't underestimating the size of my rear end.

It was going to be a tight fit.

I sensed, rather than heard, the person in the other room drawing closer. I hoisted myself up to the window and out of the corner of my eye, I saw it.

Something wedged behind the toilet. Impossible to see except from above. A large, folded-up sheet of paper.

I lowered myself and snatched it. I thrust the paper through the window and heaved myself up.

My hips jammed.

A bubble of panic rose in my throat. I knew the person in the other room must have heard me by now. I could almost feel hands grabbing at my legs and pulling me back through.

I wrenched my hips so they fit in the window diagonally. I slipped through and rolled out onto the ground. My legs thrashed in the air until I righted myself and regained my footing.

I snatched up the paper and ran all the way back to Stacy's room. I burst through the front door and locked it behind me. I collapsed on my bed.

With shaky hands, I laid down the folded-up sheet of paper. I couldn't believe I had actually stolen something from Tarzan's room. I was going to rot forever in a Costa Rican jail.

I unfolded the paper and spread it out on the bed. It was indeed a map. A topographic map, to be exact. The kind with wavy lines that shows where the terrain is flat and where it's steep.

Someone had highlighted a blue stream that wound for several miles through Piedras Blancas National Park. It ended on the coast. A black dot marked a place near the beginning of the highlighted route. I saw right away what that place was.

I pondered what the map meant. If Tarzan was traveling this route with a kayak, what was the reason?

I studied the black dot again. It was located just above the eighty-foot waterfall that Tarzan had tumbled over. The cliff would have been an impassable barrier. Perhaps he had been transporting something. If so, he may have needed to store it here until he could portage whatever it was around the fall.

I looked up from the map. Across the room, I saw something that I hadn't noticed before. Over on the floor by the front door. I had been in such a fluster when I came in that I had missed it. I tiptoed over and picked it up.

An envelope. Inside was a cryptic message from my dad:

I need to see you.
It's important.

I tossed the note aside. I went to the bed and refolded the map. Along one of the creases, I found something interesting.

A series of numbers scrawled in pen.

A phone number, perhaps? Maybe this was the number Tarzan had called the night I overheard him on the phone. Could the number belong to the bastard outfitter? Maybe the two of them had been involved in something together. Maybe they had a falling out.

Distant voices floated in from the direction of the lodge.

I needed to make a decision.

My dad wanted to see me, but I was afraid he'd interfere with my plan. I couldn't go see Anthony either. He'd been furious with me for going after Rosa. He definitely would not approve of this.

I shoved the map in the left back pocket of my shorts. Did I need to take anything else? I had been so foolish before, dashing off into the jungle without any supplies. I grabbed a scrunchie for my hair and a bottle of water.

That should do it.

I slipped out of the room before the voices could come any closer.

Once I was out-of-sight of the lodge, I tucked the bottle of water under my arm and twisted my hair up with the scrunchie. I was pleased with myself for thinking to bring the water. An adventurer is always prepared.

I slogged down a trail that I had found on the map. Hardly a few minutes had passed before the heat overwhelmed me. I stopped and took a swig of the water. I set the bottle on the ground.

It hadn't rained in a while, so the air was once again moving towards the saturation point. I shimmied out of my bra and shoved it in the right back pocket of my shorts. Once I was relieved of the underwire-fashion-demi torture device, I set off again.

I left the bottle of water by the side of the trail.

A half hour passed and I found the place marked by the black dot on the map. The place was where the trail intersected a stream. Only *stream* was the wrong word. The fast-moving water was more like a small river. Plenty big enough for a man in a kayak.

Except Tarzan's kayak was propped on his porch.

I explored the area and found nothing.

In the distance, the eighty-foot waterfall droned. I was about to give up my search when I noticed a spot where the vegetation was slightly trampled. I made my way over to the flattened area and studied the ground. Nothing was out of the ordinary. If something had been stored here, it was gone now.

Footsteps sounded down the trail.

I let out a frustrated sigh. Why did someone always have to follow me?

50

The person coming down the trail towards me was Anthony.

Relief poured over me like warm syrup. "What're you doing here?"

"Your father," he said. "He's worried about you."

"My father. He worries too much."

"He loves you," Anthony reached out a hand and curled a finger into a lock of my hair. "That's a feeling I can understand."

My eyes widened. What do you mean by that?

"I could ask the same question," he said.

"Sorry?" I felt a little panicky inside.

"What're you doing out here?" he asked.

"Oh." I turned to the spot where I had been searching. "I don't know. I thought I knew. Now, I'm not so sure." I stepped forward and peered at the undergrowth. Something looked odd.

Anthony grabbed my wrist. Spun me towards him. Trapped me with his eyes. Leaned over. Kissed me. Wrapped his arms around me. Pulled me to him. Pressed his body into mine. Held me tight.

It was a good thing he held me tight, or this time I would have toppled over without my dad's help.

My dad. What did he say about my dad?

I couldn't complete the thought. Anthony tugged at the tie that bound my hair. He pulled the unruly waves free. His words tickled my neck. "You're not wearing a bra." His voice was so low I barely heard his words though he spoke them against my ear. His closeness made me shudder.

I wobbled like a newborn foal.

Holy crap. Was I falling for this man? Well, if not, I was falling into the arms of the plants that tangled low and wild over the ground. Anthony laid me down and kissed me and I don't know if it was the earth beneath or his body above, but the scent of warmth held me close and I kissed him in return and I felt his hands like an electric blanket pulled across my neck, my shoulder, my back, my hip, my thigh.

I was finally going to taste the chocolate lava-cake. Only the molten center was in me, welling up inside my heart, searing the inside of my head, and burning somewhere low.

Anthony swirled his thumb in the space above my collar bone. "You're an amazing woman," he said.

Wow. I wanted to let go, to revel in the moment, to let it happen. But my mind would not let go.

It behaved like one of those crazy inventions at a carnival. The kind — built by some guy in his garage — with wheels and pulleys and chutes and tracks. A steel ball plunks into the top and rolls and falls and spins and shoots and winds down and over and through the contraption. With each twist and turn it sets off a new motion until the entire contraption is a whirl of activity. Then the ball plops into the last hole and you wait for it to spit out of a little tunnel at the bottom, but instead a tiny plastic penguin waddles out, drawing coos of delight from the crowd of onlookers.

I could not stop it. My mind wheeled and spun and tumbled while a cold, hard thought rolled through. When it reached the end, it shot out its own surprise.

I pushed myself up. "You said my dad's worried about me."

"Yes. What's that have to do with—"

"Where is he?"

"I don't know. He's— he's looking for you."

"How did you find me?"

"I got lucky."

"But there's a hundred places you could've gone. Why here?"

Anthony eyed me with what seemed to be wariness. "I followed you, okay?"

Something wasn't right. My dad. He left me a message. What did it say? He needed to see me right away. He'd made it clear on several occasions he didn't trust Anthony. He wouldn't have asked him for help. Wouldn't have sent Anthony looking for me. Unless he wasn't far behind. I scanned the jungle. It was like a vine-walled prison. Isolating.

I got up. The steel ball in my mind stopped rolling. Instead of a cute little penguin waddling out, a horrible enormous monster roared free.

"It was you."

"What?"

"In the dark corner."

"What're you talking about?"

"The video," I said. "Tarzan was in the lodge. He was with someone in the back. They had a map spread on the table. This map." I pulled the crinkled paper from my pocket.

The recognition in Anthony's eyes was unmistakable.

"This place. Where we're standing. It's marked on this map. I couldn't make out the other person. It was you."

"Aurora, this is crazy."

I thrashed at the jungle.

"Stop it. What're you doing?"

Something caught my attention earlier. Something didn't look right. Something was out of place. "You stopped me just now," I said. "Why? What didn't you want me to find?"

"Will you look at me for a minute?"

I looked at the jungle instead, inspecting every leaf, every vine, every tree. Just as I had focused on the leaves rattling on the mulberry tree on the day they'd come to tell me that Kaylee had hiked up the mountain to our spot — the overlook with two rocks just right for sitting — and flung herself into oblivion.

There. The plants lay a little too thickly, a little too neatly. I stepped forward.

"Aurora. Don't."

I closed my fingers around the mass of tangled vegetation and pulled. The twiny screen came free and there, arranged in tight rows and ordered stacks, were dozens of golden artifacts. Figurines and pendants and bells and beads. All grouped and sorted and tagged.

"Incredible," I said.

"Yes."

"Stolen."

"Yes."

"Why, Anthony?"

"It— it made me feel alive."

"This is what Tarzan was moving."

Anthony was silent.

"How could you?" I asked.

"What would you have me do? For years I've applied to governments. In Mexico, Honduras, Costa Rica. Applied for permission to conduct legal excavations. Waited for months. Worked through the red tape. But they only wanted to support digs in major tourist destinations."

"So to hell with the rules."

"What you have to realize, Aurora, is that every time a new site is discovered, the information leaks out to the wrong people. Then the site gets plundered. Before I — or any other archaeologist — can get a look."

"So you became the plunderer."

"A private collector came to me. He had his own museum, staff, lab, everything. He knew of a site that was supposed to exist around here. Wanted me to find it, excavate it properly. No red tape."

A thought that had ballooned up in the back of my mind popped. The realization within flooded my awareness. "Jesus," I whispered. "You killed Tarzan."

Regret flicked over Anthony's face. "Tarzan was stupid. He stole from me."

Something rustled nearby.

I turned.

Out of the corner of my eye, I saw Anthony move.

My mind performed sluggishly. Like it was trying to swim free of a bowl of jello while it thickened and set. My rational self stood by as my emotional side sought equanimity and balance.

How could I have been such a poor judge of character? Was Anthony a killer? I did not believe it. Tarzan's death must have been an accident. Or the unfortunate result of a fight. A crime of passion even.

I turned back to look at the man I had been fantasizing about for days. The man I had been flirting with every night. The man I had been kissing only moments before.

I found him standing there before me with a gun in his hand.

51

I had no idea what to do.

Run? Shout? Fight? Impossible. All of these options were impossible. The only thing I was able to do was stand and stare.

Anthony did not look at me. He did not point the gun at me. He scanned the jungle, listening.

I remembered the noise. I had to dig deep for the memory, as though the sound had occurred an eon ago, but I recalled that we had been looking at the artifacts and heard a rustle. I swiveled my head and tried to focus.

A scrap of blue fabric caught my eye.

It moved. And then I could see that it wasn't a scrap at all, but the sleeve of my dad's shirt, the one with Bozo Bear's eyes bugging out. The awful shirt that embarrassed the hell out of me whenever my dad wore it.

In Anthony's hand, the gun fired.

The sound exploded outward. The jungle absorbed the shock and soaked up every other sound with it. The earth tumbled away from under my feet. The jungle roared up in angry flames and fizzled away in a puff of smoke. The sky above boiled away to nothingness. It was just me and Anthony. Floating in a blank world.

"Daddy."

I slid backwards down a long tunnel. At the end I saw a far away version of myself beside a man with a gun. I listened to her call out. Watched the blankness close in around her.

Nausea swam in my belly. A thick fog swarmed in my head. At the end of the tunnel, the white world flickered with color.

Ice-blue water lapped on a distant shore. A girl with wild brown hair held up a fish. A man with happy eyes snapped a picture. The fish flopped, the girl squealed, the man laughed. Another image swam out of the color. The girl, older now, sat in a pile of wriggling puppies. Her dad nestled one to his cheek, smiling. The girl chose a squirmy brown one. Her dad nodded his approval. The color faded and the image dimmed into a woman crying at her best friend's funeral. The arm of her father circled her shoulders, supporting her, loving her.

As fast as they had come, the images evaporated.

Now, nothing flickered at the end of the tunnel. I had slid too far back.

Then, a strange sensation, a lifting that was somehow familiar. Strong hands on my shoulders. The tunnel twisting and warping until I was flying back out again with the world rushing back into its proper place.

My dad was there.

Whole and alive and — I understood now — shirtless.

And he was pissed.

"Aurora?" He shook me. "Snap out of it. Are you all right?"

"Dad?"

"Yes, my girl. It's me. Are you okay?"

I was so happy to see him that I wanted to hug him. Instead, I punched him in the arm.

"Ow. What the hell was that for?"

"For scaring the crap out of me."

"Out of you?"

"Yes, me. Your shirt. What were you thinking, dangling it out there like that? Like a damn target?"

"A decoy, my dear. That ridiculous blue shirt was like a damn bullseye. I didn't have time to camo up, or I'd have lost you."

"You mean — you followed me?" Hot flames jumped to my cheeks. "How long were you watching?" I feared I already knew the answer.

"Long enough." My dad moved over to the cache of artifacts. He glowered down at them with his hands on his hips.

The blurry world around me finally snapped into focus. "Anthony — where is he?"

"Gone." My dad spun on the heel of his combat boot. "Are you sure you're all right?"

"Yes, Dad. I'm fine."

"Good. Now stay here and keep an eye on this stuff."

"Wha— Why? Where are you going?"

"Anthony was right about one thing. You, my beautiful daughter, are an amazing woman. And I'm going to kill him for taking advantage of you."

That confirmed it. My dad had seen and heard everything. Sparks flew off my cheeks. I tried to say something, but words eluded me.

My dad gave me one last hard look and then — apparently satisfied that I wasn't going to keel over in a dead faint — he dashed off into the jungle.

"Dad— Wait!" I found myself talking to empty air.

Perfect. Just perfect.

Some kick-ass heroine I turned out to be. I needed my daddy to rescue me. He'd been right all along. I was no more than a helpless little girl after all. What's more, I had completely misjudged Anthony's character. I had thought he really liked me. How could he betray me like that? How could I let him? I was so stupid. I should have never come here.

I knew from that moment on the bus I was going to regret this trip. How I hated this place, with its heat and humidity and alligators and crocodiles and rivers and—

A cool hard object touched my temple.

I froze.

Damn it. I should have known. I had seen enough movies to know the villain always went down fighting. Why did I let down my guard?

Anthony must have gotten away from my dad and circled back around to me. He must have come back for his precious loot.

But if Anthony was here, then where was my dad? Could Anthony have done something to him? If he had killed Tarzan—

The barrel of the gun left my temple. A strong hand shoved me.

I stumbled forward. Tears stung my eyes. How could Anthony treat me like this? After everything we'd been through?

"*Huaquero.*"

What? I tried to turn my head.

"Do not move. Raise your hands."

That voice. I knew that voice.

It did not belong to Anthony.

52

I did as I was told. I stood still with my back to the gun and started to raise my hands.

"Now turn around. Take it slow."

I pivoted carefully, my hands raised at my sides. I found myself facing our new guide, the man Stacy was gaga over. Hector.

"*Huaquero,*" he said again.

I wondered if not moving included not talking. I decided to risk it. "What does that mean?"

"It means what you are. A robber of graves."

I slid my eyes to the cache of artifacts. "I did not—"

"You intend to blame the river guide."

So Hector knew that Tarzan was involved in this mess. Did that mean—?

"I should have realized." Hector trained the gun on me.

I eyed the barrel with apprehension. "Realized what?"

"That it was you."

"I told you. It wasn't me."

"You have much greed," Hector said.

"Greed? Me? How do you figure?"

"You tried to steal the money." He jabbed the gun towards me.

I jumped at his rapid movement.

"It is lucky," he said, "that Grace chased you away."

So he knew that I had followed him to the *escuela* that day. I wasn't as sneaky as I thought. "You knew about Grace?"

"Of course," he said. "Who do you think convinced Luis to pay the money?"

"But — why would you do that?"

"A small price for taking a child."

Understanding dawned. "You talked Grace into the whole thing. Only — in the end, she couldn't go through with it."

"I told you before," he said. "we take care of our own."

"Does taking care of your own include killing a river guide?"

Hector raised the gun a little higher.

Despite the immediate threat to my well-being, my mind raced like a background program trying to process a complex and important task. Bytes of information flowed in: The shopkeeper and Grace telling us that Hector's parents had sold their land, robbing him of his inheritance. Hector's disdain for outsiders. His defense of the Tico way of life. His impulsive behavior on the river when he rammed our raft. Add to that the passions and rashness of youth, and you had a formula for murder.

Hector stepped over to a strange tree and caressed the bark with his free hand. "You know what this is?" he asked.

"It's a tree."

"A strangler. A foreign tree that grows over another. Can you see?"

"I can see."

"A strangler moves in on an innocent tree, weaves its way into it, feeds off it, and kills it. It takes over, destroying what is already there."

"And your point is?"

"You tourists. You come here with your foreign money and your lofty ideals and you destroy people just as surely as the strangler. You think because you dress us up in costumes and make us dance that you are saving our culture. Like we are too stupid to do it ourselves. Then you trick people into selling their land instead of passing it down to their children. Just so you can come here and have your parks and your hikes and your raft trips."

Somewhere inside me, Hector hit a nerve.

Doubt wriggled through my belly. Could he be right? Was it wrong of me to do this job? Did I risk destroying this place by drawing attention to it? Had my ridiculous need to be a hero blinded me to what I was doing? I had already failed to spot Anthony's flaws.

Was I also failing to spot my own?

"You know I am right," Hector said.

I did not answer.

He went over and knelt beside the pile of artifacts. "This," he said, "is a crime. You will be brought to justice."

"I am not the one who dug those up."

"You have a convenient alibi. The river guide is dead."

"How did he die, Hector?"

"That is not your concern."

"You caught him," I said, "with the artifacts he stole."

"And now I have caught you."

"What happened to the guide, Hector?" My voice showed more boldness than I felt.

"The day of the raft trip, the guide had the gold inside the truck. Then later that same day, he came up here."

"And you followed him."

"The man was robbing graves. I had to stop him."

"And that meant killing him?"

"Confronting him. But all he had with him at the time was a paddle and a blow-up kayak. He refused to say where the gold came from."

"And you thought killing him would get him to say more?"

"It did not have to go that way." Hector's words flashed out. "The fool had a gun."

I glanced at the gun in Hector's hand. The man did not seem to find irony in the situation. "You picked up Tarzan's paddle," I said, "and you hit him."

"It did not have to go that way."

"You left him to die. You deflated his kayak and you hid it. Did it have to go that way?"

Hector shot to his feet. He narrowed his eyes at me.

I met his gaze. "You're wrong," I said.

"I am not the one who committed this crime." He stabbed a forefinger at the artifacts.

"I meant — you're wrong about tourists."

"I have seen your doubt," he said. "I saw it when I told you to write it right. I see it now."

"You're wrong, Hector. Tourists don't come here to exploit you. They come to feel and understand. Sure — they may be misguided, but you're in a position to help them learn. To help them see."

"And how," he said, "is that my job?"

"You make a choice," I said. "You can choose to let people into your life, or you can choose to shut them out. Like your pet tree over there. Maybe if it would learn to adapt, it could learn to live with the strangler."

Hector scowled. "In the meantime," he said, "should it give up and die?"

The jungle buzzed around us in anger. The sun and sky glared down with hostility. Hector and I glared at each other with contempt. We were at an impasse.

I giggled.

53

Leave it to me to behave inappropriately.

But I couldn't help it. Twenty-nine years I had lived on this earth and now within the space of twenty-nine minutes, two men had pulled two guns on me. The whole thing struck me as ridiculous.

So I giggled.

What the heck else was I supposed to do?

I was in a real mess. I had only myself to blame. This time, I wouldn't be able to rely on my daddy to rush in with his bared chest to save the day. He was busy. This was up to me.

I had to think.

What would Princess Leia and Sarah Connor and Anna Pigeon do? They'd probably whip out some Jedi moves, squash Hector until his evil red eyes winked out, or sic a pack of Yellowstone wolves on him.

And me? I skipped Jedi 101 in college, I wasn't much into squashing people, and I was definitely a long ways from Yellowstone. All I had was a bra in my pocket. Wait—

Come to think of it, I read a mystery once where the sleuth strangled a guy with her bra and then tied him up with a pair of pantyhose.

Seriously? I was in trouble.

Lucky for me, the jungle was eager for a favorable review in *See!*.

Hector menaced with the gun. He stepped forward, twisting his features and contorting his movements.

I stood transfixed. The image of Tarzan's flailing and lifeless limbs tumbled towards me over and over again. Hector could kill. Had killed. Might kill again. At any instant, the gun in his hand would retort or bash or maim or—

Get a grip. Hadn't I already been through this? The not wanting to die thing? I still had too much to see, and besides, the world was full of too many chocolate lava-cakes.

I needed to do something. I needed to live.

The jungle stepped in and created a distraction. A paca, tag dangling from its ear, twin to the creature Rosa clutched in her arms just days before, pranced out, filling the empty space between me and the man with the gun.

Hector gawped.

A branch touched the paca's tiny tush and it scurried forward and burrowed between Hector's legs.

The man squawked and danced and shook the gun at the rodenty animal. Hector's balance wavered. He wobbled, and I can't be sure, but I think the jungle stuck out a twiggy foot, causing him to trip and stumble.

The gun parted ways with his hand. It skipped through the air in a dramatic arc, skittered across a bare spot on the ground, and glinted and winked at me as it sashayed to a stop. The gun and I regarded one another. It begged me to pick it up.

It was finally happening to me. A movie moment.

The brain can do a lot of processing in a nanosecond. In that instant, it dawned on me why I was not a kick-ass heroine. It was not because I was a coward, it was not because I was weak, it was not even because I was an ordinary person instead of a character in a movie.

It was because I didn't actually want to go to war against an evil empire, I didn't want to battle inhuman terminators bent on destroying the world, I didn't want to hunt down bad guys in national parks.

I kind of liked being a person who had longings for babies, craved sleeping in, obsessed over chocolate, mooned over men, and tended to procrastinate. I kind of liked being a person who used a pen and camera to help others see.

Maybe that was heroic enough.

This realization did not change the fact that a gun lay at my feet. It did not change the fact that Hector still needed to be dealt with.

My hand went for my right back pocket.

As Hector tried to regain his balance, I lurched forward and threw my weight into his center of gravity.

Incredibly, he toppled.

Then the jungle did its part. Curled its fingers and toes and every other viny appendage around Hector's torso and limbs and held him fast.

The clasps of the bra found their way out of my pocket and into my hands. I stretched the elastic taut and pushed the undergarment over Hector's face. The two cups bulged from where his eyes tried to glare up at me.

His hands clawed at his face. I jumped up and the toe of my hiking boot cracked him where decades of legends have told me that a man can always be hurt. I guess the lore is true, for Hector's hands sped from his face to his nethers. He curled up and rolled to the side.

I whipped the 34Bs from his eyes and rolled him the rest of the way over. My knee made a dent in his back. The air whuffed out of him just long enough for me to wrench his hands together. I twisted the straps and wires and elastics around his wrists. A hand filled out each cup.

I leaped away, snatched up the taunting gun, and lobbed it into the waiting arms of the jungle where I was confident it would be tucked away from searching eyes. I had no illusions that a bit of lace would keep the man trussed for long.

So I ran away.

54

My dad ambled towards me down the main road. Shirtless. And alone.

"Dad." I rushed to him. "Are you okay?"

"Of course I'm okay," he said. "I'm combat troops."

"What happened?"

"Come with me. I'll show you." He noticed my face. "Don't worry. He's all right."

We continued in the direction my dad had come from. We reached the fork between the two roads that ran from the lodge to the village. I followed my dad down the one that led to the rickety bridge.

"Anthony had a car stashed somewhere," my dad said. "He got away from me and then I saw him flying down the main road in the car. He almost ran over some old guy with an ox. The man's cart had fallen over and blocked the whole road. I guess one of the wheels fell off."

"So Anthony was forced to go the other way."

"Yes, and he didn't make it across the bridge."

My dad and I rounded a bend and I saw it. Anthony's blue beater car. Nose down in a splintered tangle of wood.

"Are you sure he's all right?" I asked.

"Yes, I spoke to him. He's got a leg jammed. He can't get out."

"I'm sorry, Dad. I shouldn't be worrying about him after what he did to you."

"Did to me?"

"He shot at you, for crying out loud."

"Sweetie, if there's one thing I know, it's when someone's shooting at me."

"What do you mean?"

"That was a warning shot," my dad said. "High and wide."

"But I don't — why would Anthony want to warn you?"

My dad didn't answer.

"Wait a minute," I said. "He didn't know it was you, did he?"

My dad lifted his shoulders and let them drop. "There might still be someone out there who's responsible for Tarzan's death."

"So— if Anthony didn't know it was you, then that means he was trying to protect me." The wonder of that knowledge flooded through me.

My dad narrowed his eyes. "There's something you're not telling me."

There was no use hiding it. I told him what happened with Hector.

"You did what?" my dad said. "Did he hurt you? Are you all right? Why didn't you use the gun? It's not like you don't know how."

"I'm not a little girl shooting at tin cans anymore, Dad. This was real."

"All the more reason to—"

"Dad."

"All right, I'll shut up." He hooked an arm around my neck. "But — a bra? Seriously? You do read too many novels."

"And watch too many movies, I know. But now you can do what you said and shut up."

"Okay, okay." He yanked me into a hug. "I'm proud of my girl."

"Dad."

He released me. "Go." He gestured at the wrecked car.

"What? Go to him? Are you sure?"

"Just as long as you do me a favor — be careful on that bridge."

"Thank you, Daddy."

He waved me away.

I approached the car, testing each board before I put my weight on it.

Anthony leaned back on the headrest, his eyes closed. He lifted his head and opened his eyes when I creaked across the bridge. "You shouldn't be out here," he said. "It's dangerous."

"Are you hurt?" I peered into the cab. His leg was trapped in the crushed compartment beneath the steering column.

"I don't think I'm bleeding or anything. I can move my foot. I just can't get it out." He searched out my eyes. "I'm sorry, Aurora — about everything. I know I let you down."

"Well, you did take the 'hell with the rules' thing to an extreme. I'm guessing you left some details out of your reports to the dean."

"For what it's worth," Anthony said, "you made living by the rules worthwhile again."

We fell silent.

"Hey—" Anthony said.

Heat rushed to my face. "What will happen to you?"

Anthony smiled. "You mean, assuming I ever get out of this steel trap?"

I did not find humor in the situation.

"Oh, you know. An awkward international incident. I'll lose my job, there'll be jail time, fines. In a few years it'll blow over. That's provided I don't get nailed for Tarzan's death."

"That won't happen." I told him about Hector.

Emotions played across his face: disbelief, anger, concern, defeat. "Jesus," he said, "this is all my fault."

"No. No it's not. You've got to tell the police about the guy who hired you."

"That'll be difficult. I never saw him in person. He sent me the coordinates of the dig site and the location on the coast where he'd pick up the artifacts. Also a couple of guns and a few pieces of equipment."

"Sounds like he covered his own ass pretty well."

"I expect he's done this kind of thing before. But Tarzan, he was an amateur. I have no idea what he did with the items he stole."

"How many were there?"

"Just a few pieces. But they were the nicest, of course. At least I have the photos and documentation. That's something."

"Maybe I can help. I think I heard Tarzan talking to his contact on the phone one night. And I found some numbers with the map I took from his room."

"Breaking and entering? Sounds like I'm not the only crook around here."

I must have seemed worried.

"I'm not going to tell anyone," Anthony said. "It sounds to me like you've finally earned your intergalactic princess bathrobe."

Somehow that no longer appealed to me.

Loud voices drew our attention. A crowd of people, including the police officers, strode up the road towards us.

Anthony reached through the window and took my hand. "There's one man out there you can always trust."

I looked across the bridge at my dad and it occurred to me that it never was the save-the-day, be-a-hero part that appealed to me after all.

It was the part that happened after, when everyone looked around at each other and felt the connection that comes from going through something extraordinary together. From knowing the world became a little warmer, a little brighter. The sky became bluer.

The light came out of the dark.

This connection happens so seldom. It almost never happens at home where the grind of familiar patterns prevents heroic things from happening. We — all of us — want to feel special. We want to feel the glory that shines on us when we reach beyond our boundaries to grab at something greater, to live a heroic life, if only for a day or a week or a moment. This simple yearning is in us all, hardly recognizable, often only the merest hint that there is something more to us.

This is why we seek out new places, why we dream of stepping outside ourselves. It's not because we want medals and accolades, it's because we want to remember a somewhere that gave us the space to expand ourselves, to become a little more of who we truly are.

For the more places we see, the more facets of our heroic nature we can discover. A thousand angles within me waited to be seen. The clues to putting those pieces together were out there, somewhere, waiting for me to find them and create the hero I longed to be.

Even in the tallest of tales, heroes never started out that way. They were always broken, they always fell. It wasn't until the end — after they survived the journey — that they realized they didn't do it alone, that there's no such thing as heroes. Only people who step outside themselves to do what they wouldn't have done yesterday.

This possibility is in us all. It happens by the simple act of going out into the world and taking the time to see.

Even if what we see isn't always pleasant.

I shifted my attention to Anthony. "It's not about trust," I said. "It's about seeing things as they are."

"With no filter."

"Just a clear lens."

"Will you do me a favor?" Anthony asked.

"I suppose I still owe you one."

"That you do."

"Okay, then."

"Help me to see one more thing." He twirled his thumb over the back of my hand. "Your friend Kaylee — what happened to her?"

I was astounded that Anthony could think of something other than his own fate. I turned my hand in his and squeezed his palm. I told him about Cambodia. About the room.

"And the girl?" he asked.

"She didn't survive," I said. "It undid Kaylee."

Anthony lifted my hand and kissed it with a gentleness that unbalanced me. "She was very lucky to have a friend like you."

For the first time since Kaylee left, I believed it.

"Will you stay with me?" Anthony asked softly. The crowd of people had gathered at the end of the bridge.

"Yes." And I did. Until his leg was free. Until he stood on the unsteady bridge, a police officer on either side of him.

Anthony leaned in to one of the officers and asked him a question. The man glanced over at me and nodded.

Stepping forward, Anthony gathered me into his arms and held me for a long time. He pressed his lips to my hair and whispered, "Con mucho gusto."

Then the police led him away.

No longer did I think it best that Anthony was not in my life.

55

It's funny how you can go your whole life without knowing a place is out there, existing entirely independent of you. Then you visit that place and you can't imagine not knowing it, can't remember who you were before meeting the people, can't believe its stories weren't always in your memory.

I now understood why a writer with a poetic heart called this *the last country the gods made.* Costa Rica was an Eden of sorts, with its young land, flowing waters, lush fruits, varied life, heavenly spheres, and innocent children. It had snakes, to be sure, but I could see why one would find the hand of God — any god — actively at work here.

As I made my way back to the lodge, I tried to recall how I thought and how I felt before I had experienced Costa Rica.

I couldn't. It was already a part of me.

I sat in the lodge.

The other guests bustled about or relaxed in their chairs and watched the jungle's evening show. Tico crouched beside his pool, looking as though he wanted to belly up to the bar and order an *Imperial.*

In the kitchen, the cooks talked amongst themselves, their spoons clacking against metal pots and ceramic plates. Outside, the birds scolded and the bugs whined and the critters prattled. Even the late day sun made a sound as it swished over the leafy plants that shivered in the breeze.

On the first day, I had thought of the lodge as a gazebo, a static place to eat or sit or think. Now the lodge struck me as dynamic, like don Pedro's wagon wheel, with life radiating out of the center and spinning all around. Every single thing about this place was so new and rich and active and alive.

The question remained: Was I?

Stacy emerged from the kitchen. She balanced two plates in the palms of her hands. "I brought you some dessert," she said. "It'll cheer you up."

I gazed down at the plate she set before me. "How'd you know chocolate lava cake is my favorite?"

"I didn't. I asked the cooks if they could make something chocolate. Turns out, one of them is a chocoholic, too. She had a recipe from the internet she'd been wanting to try."

"Thank you."

"No problem." Stacy sat in the chair across from mine. "Hey, I heard they brought the missing paca home."

"That'll make Luis and Rosa happy."

"I also heard that the police caught Hector trying to escape through the jungle."

"I'm sorry, Stacy. I know you liked him."

"Yeah, that's okay. Rumor has it when they found him, he had a bra dangling from his arm. I guess he had a girlfriend."

I didn't want to explain that one, so I changed the subject. "You never told me what happened with the kids at the playground."

"Oh, I forgot. They told me they liked to make fun of the gringos who can't dance."

"Really?" I said. "I suppose we see what we want to see."

"Yeah," she said. "I cast those kids in the role of poor, underprivileged children. And they cast me in the role of silly white girl who can't dance. Why is it we always equate different with better or worse?"

"I don't think there's an answer to that question."

"I suppose not," she said. "So, are you going to eat that cake? Or can I have it?"

"Keep your hands off. You have your own. I'm just savoring the moment. Anticipation, after all, is the best part."

"I don't know about that," Stacy said through a mouthful of chocolate. "Eating the cake is pretty damn good, too."

I slid my spoon into the spongy dessert. The gooey center melted out onto the plate. I took a taste. The hot cocoa and sugar and butter dissolved on my tongue.

"You know something?" I pointed my spoon at the luscious cake. "I think this is what I was craving all along."

"Yeah," Stacy said. "Who needs boys anyway?"

A small sadness touched my heart.

Stacy went to the room to pack.

My dad came into the lodge. He wore a new T-shirt:

I was a sharpshooter
I got a daughter

"Jeez Dad," I said. "Nice shirt."

He hooked an arm around my neck and dragged me into a python-like embrace.

"Dad. You're hurting me."

He released me, shot out a hand, and raked his fingers through my hair.

This time...I didn't care.

"Why were you looking for me earlier?" I asked.

"You left this in the room." He handed me the palm leaf grasshopper I had created on our first night at the lodge. "Since you made this with Rosa, I figured it was important to you."

"Thanks, Dad."

He deposited himself next to me. "It's amazing," he said, "what some people will do because of a little girl."

"Yes," I said. "Or a big girl."

"A young woman."

I smiled.

"Hey," he said, "I wanted to tell you that I'm sorry about the bar stool."

I fiddled with the grasshopper's legs. One had started to slip free. "A young woman can pick herself up again."

"Yes," he said. "I suppose she can."

"So, Dad." I looked out of the lodge, towards the road that wound towards the village and ultimately, towards home. "Where do you think we'll go next?"

§

Printed in Great Britain
by Amazon.co.uk, Ltd.,
Marston Gate.